"I'M SORRY, ANDIE. I VOWED TO MYSELF I WOULDN'T let that happen."

"Why?"

He debated coming up with an excuse, anything but the truth.

He felt ashamed and brutally selfish because right then he wanted that oblivion again, with a fierce, all-consuming need.

"I don't have anything left to give you," he finally said. That, at least, was part of the truth.

Her bittersweet half smile nearly broke his heart. "I never once asked you for anything, Will."

"Andie, listen to me. You deserve better than some broken-down excuse for a cop who will never be able to give you any kind of promises."

"I don't need promises," she said, her voice barely a whisper in the night. "I don't need anything. Just you."

He should fight her, he told himself, should turn on his heel and walk into his cottage. But he wasn't strong enough. Everything in him cried out for that connection again, for the peace and solace he found only with her. He groaned even as he reached for her.

Like her ranch, she was warm and welcoming, and she sighed his name as he kissed her.

WHAT ARE *LOVESWEPT* ROMANCES?

They are stories of true romance and touching emotion. We believe those two very important ingredients are constants in our highly sensual and very believable stories in the LOVE-SWEPT line. Our goal is to give you, the reader, stories of consistently high quality that may sometimes make you laugh, sometimes make you cry, but are always fresh and creative and contain many delightful surprises within their pages.

Most romance fans read an enormous number of books. Those they truly love, they keep. Others may be traded with friends and soon forgotten. We hope that each LOVESWEPT romance will be a treasure—a "keeper." We will always try to publish

LOVE STORIES YOU'LL NEVER FORGET
BY AUTHORS YOU'LL ALWAYS REMEMBER

The Editors

Loveswept ® *833*

IN TOO
DEEP

RAEANNE
THAYNE

BANTAM BOOKS
NEW YORK · TORONTO · LONDON · SYDNEY · AUCKLAND

To Kathy Carmichael, Terry Kanago,
and the rest of the gang.
For keeping the faith.

IN TOO DEEP

A Bantam Book / April 1997

ISBN 0-553-44569-3

Published simultaneously in the United States and Canada

Bantam Books are published by Bantam Books, a division of Bantam
Doubleday Dell Publishing Group, Inc. Its trademark, consisting of the
words "Bantam Books" and the portrayal of a rooster, is Registered in
U.S. Patent and Trademark Office and in other countries. Marca Regis-
trada. Bantam Books, 1540 Broadway, New York, New York 10036.

PRINTED IN THE UNITED STATES OF AMERICA

OPM   10 9 8 7 6 5 4 3 2 1

ONE

Boring! Boring! Boring!

The word pounded into Will Tanner's head, in rhythm with the throbbing behind his eyelids, an incessant ache that three maximum-dosage, extra-strength, pain-kicking aspirin and a "Super Big Gulp" of cola hadn't been able to roust.

Throb. Boring. *Throb.* Boring. *Throb.* Boring.

He sighed, more to relieve the tedium than anything else, but his breath didn't even ripple the heavy air inside the dusty patrol vehicle.

He'd remembered western Wyoming as being beautifully cool in mid-August, a green oasis shaded from the sun by massive mountains and sheltering pines. A place worlds away from the wind-whipped, oppressive furnace of the Phoenix summertime he'd left behind not more than a week ago.

Somehow, he'd remembered wrong. Oh, sure, there were plenty of mountains around and enough pine trees to supply the world with toothpicks long into eternity. But the heat managed to ooze through their branches, settling on the stagnant air like a triple layer of electric blankets, all turned on high.

A granddaddy horsefly, drunk either with age or from the heat, buzzed slowly past the steering wheel, then perched on the open window of the vehicle before meandering to the back of Will's neck. He followed it with his eyes and even managed to summon enough energy to try shaking it off. When that didn't work, he lifted his right arm without thinking to swat it away.

Instant fire roared through his half-healed shoulder, making a mockery of the pain rattling around his head. He closed his eyes and tried to swallow his involuntary moan.

"Tanner, you're an old man," he told his white-faced reflection in the rearview mirror. "A weak, broken-down, pitiful excuse for a cop . . ."

He barely had time to start the familiar litany of curses at his own failings when static suddenly crackled through the Sheriff Department's Bronco, jolting Will and sending the elderly fly into insect shock. As he reached for the mike, the fly slammed against the windshield, then slid motionless to the dashboard.

Hell of a way to go, Will thought, before he pushed the Talk button.

"Yeah, Shirley. Tanner here. What's up?"

The static swallowed up his brand-new dispatcher's first words, but he heard, ". . . nothing much going on here, Sheriff, so I thought I'd head over to the fabric store, see if LuDene's got some of that blue cotton twill I was telling you about for my daughter's quilt. You in the middle of somethin', or can I switch any calls to your cell phone for the rest of the afternoon? Over."

He sighed again and stuck his head out the window, scanning the road ahead for some sign of action in the endless empty miles, then checking behind him. Not so much as a dust devil quaked the leaves of the aspen all around him.

"No, nothing's happening here. Shop your heart out."

"Thanks, Sheriff. Don't work too hard." He could hear her guffawing loudly in the background.

Don't work too hard. Right. In the four days since he'd been acting sheriff of Whiskey Creek, he had yet to deal with anything more troublesome than a couple of head of wayward cattle who'd knocked down a fence and stirred up a bit of trouble with some traffic. It was about as far from Phoenix as a pickle was from a jalapeño pepper.

Too much time to think, that's what he hated the most. Too damn much time to tally up all that was wrong with his life, all the stupid, tragic mistakes that had led him right here.

A late-model minivan passed his hiding place, his Bronco tucked behind a fortuitous clump of willows, and he idly aimed his radar gun at it. They weren't even going fast enough to create a breeze, he guessed, and shook his head at the reading. Forty-five in a fifty-five-mile-an-hour zone. Why didn't that surprise him? The only thing moving in the whole damn county were those hell-raising cows.

A few minutes later he saw a pickup heading toward him from the south, and the first thing he noticed about the truck was its paint job, a grimy collage of rust spots, neon pink paint, and dull gray primer.

The second thing was its speed. It rumbled past him faster than an angry bull. Will immediately shifted into gear and punched the accelerator of the Bronco, squealing rubber and spewing gravel as he rocketed onto the highway, blue and red lights flashing and his adrenaline pumping for the first time in months.

The grand chase was over almost before it began. As soon as the driver glimpsed his lights, the battered pickup was obediently pulled to the side of the road. Hell, he thought. The first time in four days he felt like more than a windbreak, and he didn't even get a chance to kick up a little dust.

Still, instinct and bitter experience lent caution to his actions as he left the patrol vehicle and carefully approached the driver's side of the pickup. He slipped his sunglasses into the breast pocket of his uniform and, one hand resting over his Glock, took quick notice of every identifying detail of the truck.

The license plate—Wyoming LC 4506.

The make—an ancient Chevy, probably late fifties, early sixties.

One bumper sticker: Think Globally, Act Locally.

The door suddenly flew open, and Will had a swift impression of bare arms and legs.

"Stay where you are!" he commanded, his harsh words echoing in the motionless air. The figure half out of the truck started to climb back in. "I said, stay where you are," he barked again, commanding instant obedience.

"Now, climb out real slow. Keep your hands where I can see them."

A husky laugh wafted across the heat waves shimmering off the pavement, but seconds later a woman in khaki shorts and a maroon T-shirt hopped to the ground, waving her hands dramatically.

"You caught me, Sheriff. I was just about to head for the border with my illegal load of manure, but you've spoiled all my dastardly plans." She had a whiskey-rich voice, this speeder of his, Will thought, even as he tried to ignore the glimmer of masculine interest the combination of a sexy voice and bare limbs ignited in him.

"Do you know how fast you were traveling, ma'am?" he asked instead.

She laughed again, sending another trickle of awareness sneaking through him. "You can take your hand off your weapon there, Sheriff Tanner. Trust me, I won't try to wrestle you to the ground for it." She held up three fingers. "Scouts' honor."

She was far from a Boy Scout. No bigger than five foot three, she was slim but not scrawny. Thick shoulder-length dark hair curled around her face, and deep green eyes glimmered with laughter. A fine layer of dust coated tanned skin, in stark contrast to both the delicateness of her features and the three tiny diamonds glittering in each of her ears.

"And, to answer your question," she went on, "no, I don't have any idea how fast I was going. The speedometer in the Beast has never worked, at least not in my lifetime."

"Which is all of, what, eighteen years?" he asked

before he could stop himself. Damn, he felt old next to all her bubbling energy.

The woman just laughed once more. "Aren't you a sweetheart? And you've got such a reputation for being a grouch too!" She extended a sun-kissed hand to him. "I'm Andrea McPhee, and last month I had thirty-two whole candles on my birthday cake."

Before he could stop himself, he was reaching for her hand, feeling an odd mix of calluses and softness. It unnerved him, and if there was one thing he hated, it was being unnerved.

"Will Tanner." He introduced himself gruffly, snatching his hand back.

"I know who you are." Andrea McPhee smiled winsomely at him. "Sheriff William Charles Tanner, thirty-six, father of Emily who's eleven going on twenty-five, I understand. You're a native Wyomingite, from over near Star Valley way, who hasn't been back in years. You have a master's degree in criminology and are on loan from the Phoenix vice squad while you recuperate from a 'job-related injury,' a polite way of saying a nasty gunshot wound. As far as anyone can tell, you don't have any hobbies, at least you haven't for the past few years."

She paused in the recitation as Will felt fury growling to life inside him.

"You really should learn to relax, Sheriff," she continued, "or you're going to have a heart attack just like your predecessor."

"How do you know all that about me? Does the whole damn county know my life story?"

She laughed again. And again, it slid down his

spine like a silky caress, despite his anger at having his life so exposed.

"Simmer down, Sheriff. Your secrets are safe. I'm good friends with your sister. Beth has been raving about her wonderful older brother since the day I met her, and . . ."

Her voice trailed off, and she gave him a hard look. "Should you be standing out here in the sun, in your condition?" Even as she spoke, she was leading him to the shade of a huge pine that flanked the road.

He didn't even realize he'd followed her like a puppy after a bone until he felt a welcome breeze drift across his sweat-soaked skin.

"Yeah," he said stubbornly, and headed toward his Bronco, leaving the blessed coolness behind. "In the sun is exactly where I should be, especially when I'm giving tickets to nosy people who apparently think they're above the law."

He sounded childish and it made him even angrier, but he forced himself to calmly grab his clipboard and a pen out of the Bronco. He turned back to face her truck just in time to find her half inside it, reaching across the seat.

Will nearly dropped the clipboard in the dust.

The khaki shorts, which had looked perfectly modest when she was standing in front of him, now rode up the backs of her thighs as she bent over, making her tanned, shapely legs look about a mile long. He swallowed hard against a suddenly parched throat and ordered himself to look away.

When was the last time he'd responded so physically to a woman? Months? Years? *Ever?*

"At least let me get you something to drink while

you're writing up my ticket," she called from inside the truck, her voice muffled.

"Your license and registration would be sufficient."

Even though he tried hard not to look at her, he was aware of her backing out, holding two sodas. Ice chips clung to the shiny aluminum, and little beads of condensation gleamed in the harsh sun. The can she was holding out to him was the most enticing thing he'd ever seen, next to the delicious woman herself.

If his years of police work had given him anything beyond bone-deep cynicism and weary resignation, it was a healthy dislike of things he couldn't control. The murky hell of the past three years had done nothing to ease that. Why, then, was he letting her creep beneath his skin?

"Here, take it," she urged, moving closer to him. She smelled of lavender and woman, and Will forgot to breathe. "You can't be too careful in this heat, especially when you're already fighting your injuries."

"I'm not some damn invalid," he snapped, backing away from her, trying to return to some semblance of a comfort zone. "And you're not my friggin' babysitter, lady."

"If I were, I'd wash your mouth out with soap and make you sit in the corner until you stopped acting like a five-year-old," she snapped back. "It's not going to kill you to take a little drink."

"Back off."

She shrugged. "Fine. Be that way." To his dismay, she opened one of the cans and put it to her mouth, exposing a long, graceful neck as she tilted her head back to drink. He suddenly wanted a taste so badly he could almost feel the cool liquid bubbling down his throat, but he'd rather be staked out naked on an ant-hill than ask her for it.

"Sure you don't want some?" She held the other can out.

Will growled. "Is there any other way to shut you up, so I can do my job?"

She shook her head, and he sighed. He snatched the can from the woman, jerked it open, and took a long drink as if he'd, indeed, been staked out in the scorching sun for the last three months.

"You're welcome," she said sweetly.

Guilt assailed him. She'd done nothing to deserve his miserable mood. It certainly wasn't her fault she'd somehow managed in only a few minutes to thaw nerve endings he'd thought permanently frozen.

"Sorry," he muttered. "Thank you."

"Rough day?" she asked.

He fingered the soda. "I'm just having a tough time getting used to all this . . . nothing . . . again."

She laughed, low and genuine. "I know, it can be a bit overwhelming. The first winter I moved here from St. Louis I nearly went stir-crazy from the slow pace. Now I get that same edgy, out-of-control feeling whenever I go back to the city to visit. Odd how a few years can change you so much."

Yeah, well, he wouldn't be here that long, Will thought, swallowing the last of his drink. Just a few months and he'd be back in the middle of it all.

With that in mind, he set the can on the hood of her truck and finished documenting her ticket.

"Here you go, ma'am." He handed her a copy of the citation. "See that you fix your speedometer. You wouldn't want to plow into any stray cattle going that fast."

She laughed and tucked the ticket into the pocket of her T-shirt, then tossed his can into her truck before climbing in after it. He forced himself to look away until she was settled on the high seat.

"Okay, Sheriff. I'll be sure to do that. Nice meeting you."

He nodded and walked back to his brown-and-white Bronco. Andie watched him go in her side-view mirror, releasing a shaky sigh and swatting a wayward strand of hair away from her face.

"Oh, Beth," she said out loud. "The things you conveniently forgot to mention about your dear big brother could fill a book."

She glanced in the mirror again as she buckled her seat belt and worked the Beast's gear shift into neutral so she could start it. The new sheriff stood beside his patrol vehicle, one foot perched on the fender while he filled out paperwork, using his jeans-clad knee for a desk.

He must not have realized she was looking at him, because he paused to massage his right shoulder with his left hand, a grimace tightening those hard, sharp features. Sunlight glinted off his thick brown hair, and she could see traces of auburn and a few almost-hidden sprinkles of silver.

Tall, with a rangy cowboy's build—all shoulders and lean hips—he was rough and male. And very, very appealing.

"Scratch that, Beth," Andie went on. "The things you conveniently forgot to tell me about your dear big brother could fill the whole blasted Library of Congress."

It was his eyes, though—the silvery gray of a wolf's sleek winter pelt—that were so compelling. He'd tried to hide it, but she'd been able to see the bruised pain in them, the irresistible look of a battered and wounded soldier.

Irresistible to some women, she reminded herself as she drove away. Not to her. Never to her. She had enough causes in her life.

She had absolutely nothing left to offer a man who looked like he desperately wanted rescuing but would snap out like an injured bear if someone were foolhardy enough to offer a helping hand.

The thought unaccountably depressed her, but Andie shrugged it off as she traveled the last few miles to her ranch. Instead, she turned her attention to the million things she had to do before she could hit her pillow that night.

The phone was ringing as she slid out of the truck. She could hear it from the open kitchen window, even over the combined babble of one goat, two dogs, five cats, and a dozen chickens trying to grab her attention.

"Just a sec, guys." She laughed as she tried to make it to the door through the throng of animal bodies without stepping on any tails or tail feathers.

Just before she reached the phone, Andie paused. Would it be her friendly little breather again? she wondered as a tiny chill of fear crept across her skin. The one who had been calling regularly for the past few months, whispering threats and dark promises for a "busybody little schoolteacher"?

She had absolutely no intention of running like a

scared mouse every time the phone rang, she told herself, and picked up the receiver.

"Andie, I've been trying to call you for hours," the voice on the other end said. "I was just about to drive over to see if you were up to your elbows in dirt out in the garden and couldn't hear the phone."

Andie dropped her packages and slumped into one of the kitchen chairs with more relief than she cared to admit. An image of silver-gray eyes flashed through her mind as she greeted the new sheriff's sister.

. "Hi, Beth. How's my favorite mother-to-be?"

"Big as a barn," her friend responded cheerfully. "And about ready to climb the walls of that big ol' red one outside. You sure I can't come back to work?"

"Absolutely not. As much as I need my assistant director, you don't need to be dealing with thirty rambunctious preschoolers right now."

"Well, Jace won't let me so much as hang a picture. He's driving me nuts, Andie. If I didn't have Emily over here, I'd have been out in my own garden, but I'm afraid she'd take great delight in getting me in trouble by tattling on me."

Andie smiled. She had yet to meet Beth's niece, but according to her friend, the eleven-year-old was a real handful.

"I know you don't want to hear it," Andie said, "but Jace is right. You can't be too careful with that baby of yours." She couldn't help the spasm of old pain that twisted her heart, but she was proud of herself for keeping any of it out of her voice. "You've waited long enough for her that these last few months will go by fast."

"I can always count on you to keep life in perspective," Beth said fondly. "Which reminds me. I need a really, really, really big favor."

"Anything," Andie said, and meant it. No favor she could do for the other woman would repay Beth for the past five years of friendship.

"It's about my brother Will," Beth continued. "I told you he'd planned to rent Ruby Miller's house on the other side of town for the three months he's going to be here, but now her son has changed his mind. He says he wants to get the thing ready so he can sell it. Greedy little snot didn't even wait until Ruby was cold before selling off all her prized possessions. So I've been frantically trying to find somewhere else for him to live."

"For Ruby Miller's greedy little snot of a son?"

"No, silly. For Will and Emily. Do you realize we have no rental property around here? At least nothing decent. It's absolutely disgusting, if you ask me. Anyway, while I was sitting here moping around I had this brilliant idea. Don't say no until you think about it, okay?"

"Until I think about what?"

"Could you possibly let Will and Emily live in the cottage? I know you like to save it for your mom to stay in when she visits, but she was just here and you said she's not coming back until next spring. It's only for a few months, Andie, Christmas at the latest, and you wouldn't even know they were there, I swear. Please, please, please."

Stunned, Andie could do nothing but clutch the phone. Will Tanner in the same county was trouble enough, but to have him living just across the driveway would be close to catastrophic.

"Beth, I don't . . . I don't think it would work."

"Why not? It's perfect. You know how I worry about you living out there by yourself. Wouldn't it be a comfort to have the law right next door?"

A comfort? Andie almost laughed, despite her shock. It wouldn't be a comfort in the least, not when "the law" was Will Tanner.

"I don't think we'd get along."

She could practically hear Beth's frown transmitting itself through the telephone wires.

"How do you know? You've never even met the man."

"Wrong. He pulled me over not an hour ago cruising sixty-five in a fifty-five zone. We didn't exactly hit it off."

"I know he can be a bear sometimes, but he's really a sweetheart beneath all that gruff. Or at least he used to be," she added, her voice breaking halfway through the sentence. Beth paused for a moment, then continued. "Andie, I really am in a bind. Every morning my heart just breaks when I see Will try to hide how much sleeping on that awful couch is killing his shoulder. If this goes on much longer, I'm going to let him use our bed, no matter what that husband of mine has to say about it."

Andie closed her eyes, momentarily furious at Will Tanner. Beth didn't need this anxiety right now. She was in the last two months of what had been a dangerous, strenuous pregnancy. She needed calm and quiet, time to gather her strength before delivery.

"He might not like it, you know," she said, realizing she'd already given in. "You know how small that place is." And Will Tanner was the kind of man who looked like he needed acres of space to sprawl around in.

"It's furnished, it's clean, it's convenient. Plus he gets a gorgeous landlady like you. What more could a man ask for?"

Andie grimaced in defeat. "If he wants to take a look at it, tell him to drop by the school tomorrow to pick up the key."

"Oh, Andie, thank you. Thank you! You do this for me and I'll name my baby after you, I promise."

Andie hung up the phone and walked slowly back across the kitchen. The hinges need oiling, she thought as she opened the squeaky screen door. Just one more thing to add to her list.

She let the door slam closed behind her and looked across the yard at the guest house just a few hundred feet away.

What have I done? she wondered, slumping down on the front porch step. Immediately, both dogs and two of the cats cuddled up looking for affection, and she absently scratched whatever fur was closest.

"Well, guys," she warned the menagerie. "There goes the neighborhood."

TWO

"If Aunt Beth wants us out of her house so bad, why don't we just go back to Phoenix? Wyoming bites the big one!"

Will clenched his fingers on the steering wheel and frowned at his daughter. She glared back at him, chewed her gum hard, and folded her arms across her chest, a mutinous expression twisting her little-girl features.

How had his sweet, easygoing daughter grown into such a wild and angry rebel as she teetered on the brink of teenagehood? he wondered for the umpteenth time.

"You know why, Emily," he said patiently. "I have a job to do here for the next three months."

"Right. *You* have a job to do. Meanwhile, I'm stuck in the middle of Hicksville, Wyoming, without my friends or a mall or even MTV. It absolutely sucks. All because you were stupid enough to get yourself shot, and now you can't cut it as a cop in the city."

"Watch it, young lady," he growled, even though

what she said was nothing less than the truth, at least for the moment. "You're not too big that your stupid old dad can't turn you over his knee and teach you a few manners."

Despite the fact that he'd never laid a hand on her in anger during her entire eleven years, the threat seemed to work, at least temporarily. As he drove the last few miles from Beth and Jace's ranch, the Bar W, to the town of Whiskey Creek, she sat silent and sullen, staring out at the passing pines.

She'd been this way—angry, confrontational—for three months, ever since he'd been shot. Or maybe it had been longer than that, he admitted with a painful jolt, and he just hadn't seen it. He hadn't bothered to look until being knocked flat on his butt had forced his eyes wide open.

Where had he been while his little girl's interests had changed from dolls to boys? When had she stopped calling him Daddy with a world of innocent love in her voice and begun regarding him with such apparent contempt?

What had been so damned important to him that he missed out on so much of her life in the past three years?

Vengeance.

The word, brutal and fierce, pounded through the fragments of headache lingering from the day before.

Vengeance.

It ate away at his calm, leaving him edgy, uneasy. Sarah's face haunted him on the rim of his vision, beautiful and beseeching, before he quickly blinked it away. He forced himself to relax his fingers on the steering wheel and fill his lungs with air.

His chance would come, Will reminded himself. He was close, achingly, agonizingly close. He only needed time, a few months to build up his strength. Then he could return to finish it.

Time to heal. It was the only reason he was smack in the middle of Hicksville, Wyoming, as Emily called it. Either he could have taken the temporary sheriff job when his old buddy Hank Martinez called and asked for his help after a heart attack laid Hank up, or he could have sat in their house in Phoenix and watched Emily grow up and away from him.

Hank had been one of his instructors at the Wyoming police academy what seemed a lifetime ago. He'd retired several years back to the slower pace of Whiskey Creek, but had been sidelined a month earlier. All three of his deputies were greenhorns he wouldn't trust with a jaywalker, he'd said when he called from his hospital bed, so would Will take over until Hank was back on his feet?

It had seemed the perfect solution, even if, as Will suspected, Beth had been the one behind the idea. He'd been at loose ends since his bosses in Phoenix were still angry at him. They didn't take kindly to one of their officers getting in a shootout while working on a case he wasn't supposed to even be close to.

Beyond the probation he'd gotten that would extend for another few months, they also wouldn't let him into the station house until his shoulder healed completely, unless he wanted to take a damn desk job.

Percolating underneath the desire for something useful to do while he recovered was a hope that if he could wean Emily away from whatever shady influences she'd begun to run with, he might be able to break through her brittle shell. Somewhere in there was the little girl who used to fling arms smelling of baby powder around him and nuzzle her face into his neck.

Crowding into his sister's house hadn't helped their relationship any, though, he admitted. He'd been just about to tell Beth he wanted to find a place of their own for these few months when she told him about her friend's ranch three miles from the Bar W.

"It has this perfect little two-bedroom cottage on it, apart from the main place," she'd gushed during breakfast that morning. "It was the main ranch house once years ago, and then when the other house was built it was used for a foreman's place. Since the ranch doesn't support many animals now, just a few chickens and an ornery little goat named Mr. Whiskers, there's no foreman anymore. Just Andie and that little zoo."

With Beth's typical mercurial change of emotion, her enthusiasm veered into concern. "You don't feel like I'm pushing you out, do you? If it were just the baby, Will, I'd love to have you stay even if we had to decorate the nursery three months from now and have her sleep in a dresser drawer until it's finished. But I can't stand that you're in pain, and I just know that couch is killing you."

"Don't fuss, Beth. I'm okay," he answered gruffly.

"Horse pucky. This is your little sister you're trying to fool here and I'm not buying it. A man your size, even without your injuries, needs a big bed to stretch out on, not some teensy couch."

He sighed. Beth had been able to twist him around her little finger since long before their parents' deaths had made him her guardian. Fifteen years hadn't changed anything.

"I'll look at it, okay?"

"That's terrific. You're a doll." She threw her arms around him, and he barely managed to hide his wince when she jostled his shoulder.

"I talked to Andie about it yesterday, and there's no problem with you taking a look at it today. I'll just write the address down where you can pick up the key. You'll love it, I promise!"

Will had his doubts. Nothing about this temporary job had been as he expected. Including the address where Beth told him he could find this Andy Something-or-other.

He shoved the Jeep gear into park and stared at the building he'd stopped in front of. With wood siding and a shake roof, it looked like many of the newer buildings in town, but a playground adjacent to it, the swings swaying in the wind, set it apart. A big sign out front blared its name in rainbow colors: Growing Minds Preschool.

When they walked inside, Will had a quick impression of a child's wonderland. Bright and colorful, with skylights and big windows, the schoolroom was filled with things to stimulate a child's imagination: blocks and books and paints. Miniature furniture was scattered around the room in little conversation nooks. A real live tree grew up in the center of the room, reaching for one of the skylights, and lush, ferny plants in the corners gave the room a jungle feeling. There was even a porch swing hanging inside, covered with plump pillows and storybooks.

"Wow! What a cool place," Emily exclaimed, her

face glowing with more excitement than he'd seen in weeks. As soon as she met his gaze, the delight slid away to be replaced by the bored mask she favored of late. "I mean, if you're into that kind of lame baby stuff."

Two dozen preschoolers, giggling and munching cookies, sat in a half circle around a wooden structure that looked like a square playhouse with a ladder leading up to a loft on the roof. A puppet show was going on, with a large window in the playhouse serving as a stage.

Three women sat in chairs behind the children, and he walked over to them.

"Excuse me," he said in a loud whisper to the closest one. "I'm looking for somebody named Andy. Am I in the right place?"

"Shhh," the woman admonished him.

Impatient, he frowned but slid onto a chair to wait for the show to end. After a few minutes, he had to admit it was cute. Even earned a rusty smile or two from him.

He spied Emily laughing right along with the younger kids, and felt an ache lodge in his chest. Lord, he missed that sweet little girl she used to be.

The show ended to the laughing applause of the children, and the narrator ducked out of the small house to take a bow. Will's jaw dropped.

It was his speeder, Andrea McPhee. She looked like a completely different woman, though, in a trim navy skirt and striped T-shirt. With her mop of curly dark hair held back with a scarf and pearl earrings, she looked prim and proper and worlds away from the tanned, dusty siren of the day before.

Bracelets jangling, she reached down to hug a black-haired girl and high-fived a tough-looking boy all in the same motion. Will could tell when she spied him because her eyes widened, then narrowed. She slowly straightened, disengaging herself from the crowd of children, and walked to him.

"Sheriff Tanner," she greeted him, smiling. "I hope you haven't come to arrest me. I paid my ticket just this morning, honest!"

That undertone of throaty laughter annoyed him for some elusive reason. He stood abruptly. "I'm here to find somebody named Andy. Is he here?"

Again that subtle laughter floated from her. "No, he's not. She is."

For a moment, he faltered. He could swear Beth had referred to Andy as a man, but then he hadn't really been paying much attention.

"Fine," he said abruptly. "Where is she?"

She smiled, revealing a dimple on one side of her mouth. It zeroed right into his gut, making him even surlier.

"You've found her."

He stared. "You're Andy? The one I'm supposed to be renting a house from?"

"Isn't life just a kick in the seat?" She was openly laughing at his disbelief now as she led the way to a cramped little office overflowing with more books and plants and toys.

"Right. A real kick."

He couldn't possibly rent a house from her, Will thought as he stood in the doorway watching her dig through a huge straw bag. Besides this odd and uncomfortable awareness that seeped under his skin when he was near her, he didn't think he wanted a landlady who found such obvious enjoyment at his expense.

"Sorry to have bothered you," he said stiffly. "Beth said you don't normally rent the house out. I'm sure you don't want to make an exception in my case."

"It's no bother."

"We'd probably be terrible tenants."

She laughed again. "That's okay. I'm probably a terrible landlady too. We nosy types who think we're above the law usually are."

Had he really said that to her? he wondered. Just another reason why he needed to convince her they wouldn't suit.

"I mean, with my job, I might be coming in and out at all hours of the day and night." He clenched a fist at his side. "Hell, even when I am home at night, I usually don't sleep well. And then there's Emily. I could tell her not to bother you, but she probably still would."

"What do you want me to say, Sheriff? That I've changed my mind and I'm no longer willing to rent to you?"

"Yeah," he growled. "That's exactly what I want you to say."

"Sorry," she returned blithely. "I'm not going to make it that easy on you."

"Why not?"

Her smile tightened. "Look, Sheriff, I don't give a flying fig about you and your late nights and your erratic hours. The only person in this I care about is Beth. She's my friend. For the first time in five years she has asked me for a favor, and I'm going to do everything in my power to grant it, even if it means putting up with her ungrateful oaf of a brother for a few months."

She wound down and drew in a deep breath. "Take the key. If you think the place will work, you will darn well move in. Got it?"

He watched her wordlessly for a few beats, then snatched the key from her hand.

"Fine," he snapped. "Don't say I didn't warn you."

Don't say I didn't warn you.

Andie thought of his ominous words as she drove into her gravel driveway four hours later.

An unfamiliar Jeep Cherokee, its hatch open and overflowing with boxes, waited in front of the foreman's house to be unloaded.

Looks like she had herself a tenant.

What had she gotten herself into? The last thing she needed was an ornery bear of a man crowding into her space, watching her suspiciously out of those tormented, weary, beautiful eyes. Stirring up feelings she'd thought long dead, buried so deep within her they'd crumbled away into nothing.

Still, it was too late to back out now, especially after she'd all but ordered the man to move in.

She had a sudden, fierce longing to escape into her gardening clothes and hide away among her herbs, to repair her shattered composure amid the hum of honeybees and the gentle dance of columbines.

Surely these past five years had made her more adept at handling confrontations. But at the first sign of trouble, here she was wanting to run away again.

Not this time, she thought. She slammed her car door and resolutely marched up the back porch steps and rapped on the old wood door.

When Will answered, wariness flickered in his eyes, the color of the sky just before a summer squall. He said nothing, just watched her from behind the screen.

"May I come in?" she asked.

He shrugged and held open the door. "It's your house."

"For the next few months, it's yours." She tried a smile, uncomfortably aware of the current sizzling between them as she slipped past him into the kitchen. That summer storm came to mind again, all lightning and superheated air and distant rumblings.

She cast off the fanciful thought. "After Beth called me yesterday, I turned on the power and lit the pilot light for the water heater. I'm afraid there's no air conditioner, but it only stays hot in here from about noon to four. The ceiling fans should help until it cools down in the evening. We only have a few more weeks of summer weather, anyway."

"We'll be fine."

The cottage seemed smaller somehow with him there, Andie thought, as if the walls had shrunk around him. It even smelled different than it had when she'd been there that morning. Of cedar and pine. Rugged and rough.

What had she gotten herself into?

She took another steadying breath and glanced at Will, who leaned back against the kitchen counter, his arms folded.

"Where's Emily? I'm eager to meet her."

"Beth's. She said something about some show she wanted to see tonight. Since we don't have a television out here yet, she decided to stay there one more night."

A civil sentence out of the man, Andie thought, suppressing a grin. What was the world coming to? "You know," she said, "I've got two over at the house and I rarely watch either one of them. You're welcome to use one, if you'd like."

"Thanks." His jaw worked, as if it hurt him to say the word.

"It will just take me a minute to dig it out."

Coward, she called herself as she walked across the driveway to her own back door. She hadn't even been near Will Tanner for two minutes and here she was seizing on the most pitiful excuse she could find to escape.

She found the television set, still in its box, in her spare room. She hefted it into her arms and after sidestepping the eager animals who'd suddenly realized she was home, she made it to his back door.

"Sheriff?" she called through the screen.

He opened the door and she carried the box to the kitchen table.

"I can't promise the reception will be wonderful out here in the boondocks, but somebody who lived here before me rigged up an antennae on top of the barn. We usually get three or four channels, unless it's raining."

"That should be fine," he said gruffly.

"Where would you like it? The living room?" She grabbed the box from the table at the same moment he reached for it from the other side. Their hands touched, and just for an instant, electricity arced between them. The jolt shook her clear to her toes, and Andie could swear the air crackled and sparked between them.

Their gazes met, and she saw burgeoning awareness in his gray eyes before he turned abruptly, jerking the box out of her hands.

"I can take it. Thanks for bringing it over."

It was a clear dismissal, Andie thought, still shaken from the brief, sizzling contact. If she had a lick of sense, she would just head back over to the safety of her side of the driveway. As the full weight of the box fell into his arms, though, she saw pain flit across his features before he headed into the other room.

What was it about men? Was there some sort of stubbornness gene imprinted on the Y chromosome, some hidden marker that dictated they must, at all costs, pretend they were welded out of tough, unbreakable iron?

Andie shook her head and headed to the Jeep. She would just carry in a few of the bigger boxes, she told herself. It was the neighborly thing to do, after all. She might not have learned much about handling confrontations since coming to Whiskey Creek, but she had learned the value of being a good neighbor.

She was on her second load when he rolled back into the kitchen. He stopped abruptly and glowered at her from the doorway. "What the hell do you think you're doing?"

"Tap dancing. What does it look like?" She laughed at his frown. "I'll carry the rest of the boxes in and you can put things away. It should only take us a few minutes if we work together."

"I didn't ask for your help, lady, and I damn well don't need it."

"You didn't ask. I'm offering."

"I don't need a nursemaid." He snatched the box from her and hauled it through the doorway to the living room.

"Good grief," Andie exclaimed, trailing after him. "I'm just trying to help you bring in a few boxes, to save a little wear and tear on your shoulder. I'm not offering to give you a sponge bath, for heaven's sake."

"Get this through your head. You're my landlady; I'm your tenant. That's it. We're not friends, and you're sure as hell not my mother. I'll pay my rent on time and you just stay out of my way and we should get along fine."

Andie studied him for a moment, noting the tight lines of pain around his mouth and the stiff set of his shoulder.

Good grief. Still, she'd made the effort. It was nothing to her if the man worked himself back into the hospital, was it?

"Fine." She shrugged, heading toward the door. "Knock yourself out."

She scrupulously avoided looking out her windows at her new neighbor as she changed into gardening clothes and made a sandwich and salad for dinner. It wasn't until she was filling the dogs' dishes by the kitchen door that she caught a glimpse of Will walking out for what appeared to be the last load from the Jeep.

He hefted a big box, and even from thirty feet away she could see him wince.

Good grief.

In a few minutes, despite the strident arguments of all her better instincts, she was knocking on his door again. Will opened it, a scowl creasing his forehead.

"What now?"

She held out a jar of ointment. "Rub this on your shoulder if the pain starts getting to you."

He studied the jar suspiciously but unscrewed the lid and took a whiff. "What is it?"

"A little of this, a little of that. Mostly mountain laurel—nothing that should kill you. It's an old family recipe."

She hopped down the steps and was halfway across the driveway when he called after her. She pivoted back. "Yes?"

Studiously avoiding her gaze, he fingered the door knob. "Thanks. And, uh, sorry for snapping at you back there."

Her smile was genuine. "You're welcome."

Andie tried to avoid thinking about Will while she spent the rest of the evening digging in her garden. It wasn't an easy task. She'd become accustomed to being alone, to walking around in her bare feet, to singing off-key at the top of her lungs if she felt like it. Even though she didn't see him again, she couldn't shake the feeling of invasion just knowing he was over in the foreman's cottage.

Later—after she'd soaked in the tub and climbed into bed—she gave up the struggle and let her mind wander over all the bits and pieces she knew about him. Really, thanks to Beth those bits and pieces added up to quite a clear picture of Will Tanner. Her friend had never been hesitant to talk about him, and Andie, oddly enough, had been intrigued about the man long before she met him, before she discovered he had a warrior's build and a devil's face, all hard planes and angles.

She knew his wife had been killed a few years earlier. Beth had taken several weeks off work to fly to Phoenix and help Will with his daughter, and she'd come back withdrawn and devastated by her brother's grief.

Andie knew he'd immersed himself in his work since then.

And she knew every grisly detail about the gun battle that had wounded him three months earlier and resulted in the death of one of the men involved in his wife's murder. And that the man who had masterminded the whole thing—the one who had shot both his wife and, later, Will—had escaped once again.

What she didn't understand was why he fascinated her so much. Why the few times she'd seen him, her pulse seemed to accelerate like she was hiking up the face of Lone Eagle Peak. Why she had a terrible fear he was going to completely jumble up the careful order she'd created of her life.

She fell asleep still wondering.

The phone's insistent ring woke her, and dragged her out of an unsettling dream about shootouts and wounded sheriffs, Andie glanced at the clock to find it was a few minutes past midnight.

"Hello?" She cleared the sleep from her voice.

Nobody answered. Her tormenting caller, she realized. He'd been calling every few weeks all summer long, sometimes in the middle of the night, sometimes early in the morning. One unnerving time at the school. Always when her guard was down.

She could hear him there now, taunting her with his silence, and she was just about to slam the receiver down when that voice—that oddly garbled, eerie mockery of a voice—whispered to her.

"Mind your own business, little schoolteacher."

The message was almost always the same. And so was her response. It had become sort of a sick game between them.

"No," she said as calmly as she could, and very gently replaced the phone in its cradle.

For a long time she sat there in bed, holding the pillow tight against her chest. She wasn't exactly scared, she told herself, just unnerved a bit. Still, she couldn't help creeping to the window and taking a careful look around her property.

All seemed in order. The dogs were quiet. In fact, the only noise was the barn owl calling to its mate and a loose section of metal roof on the drying shed pinging in the breeze.

Scaredy cat, she chided herself, and was ready to climb back into bed when a dark shadow disengaged itself from the trunk of the huge old limber pine that gave the ranch its name.

Andie's heart skipped a few beats, and she stepped back out of view until she realized the dogs would have raised one heck of a ruckus if a stranger were near. As the figure moved into the pale moonlight, she gave a shaky sigh of relief when she recognized Will Tanner.

For a long time, she watched, puzzled, while he walked the whole length of the ranch, turning his head back and forth, as if looking for something. It wasn't until he was out of sight on the other side of the house and she had climbed back into bed that the explanation for his odd behavior struck her.

Just like that wounded soldier she'd imagined him to be, he was checking out the perimeters of his new territory, examining every inch of the ranch, checking to make sure all was in order before he settled in for the night.

Despite her lingering unease from the phone call, Andie lay in her bed for a long time twisting her fingers into the scalloped edge of her old wedding ring quilt and smiling into the dark.

THREE

This was all she needed, Andie thought, carefully cutting a sprig of lemon thyme to add to the others in her basket.

Other women might long for money or high-powered jobs or successful husbands. Her dreams, however, were right here: the gentle balm of the early morning sun, the cool dirt between her fingers, the smell of lavender and sage thick in the air.

To her, it was paradise, more precious still because of the battles—both emotional and physical—she'd fought to claim it.

She sat back on her heels and gazed around her little corner of the world. The barn and drying shed gleamed white in the morning sun. Hummingbirds and bees and kaleidoscopic butterflies flitted among the brilliant flowers. The water in the irrigation ditch that separated the garden from the house bubbled and gurgled in a familiar, comfortable song.

It was homey and welcoming. And it was hers.

When she stumbled on the ranch five years earlier,

it had been barely livable, the garden fallow, the buildings literally toppling down. From the very beginning, though, the place had called to her.

In an odd sort of way, the ranch *was* her. Its rebirth had been her rebirth. Its healing, her healing.

She'd needed to work, then. Hard work. Strenuous, cleansing labor. She'd poured every ounce of her strength into the place, and later into the preschool.

As a result, Limber Pine Ranch sparkled and gleamed, its orchard ripe with fruit, its gardens productive once more. And the school had proved a success beyond her wildest dreams, drawing children from low-income families all across the county.

It was enough, she told herself. If sometimes she still lay in her bed at night and felt she would disappear under the weight of her loneliness, well, it was nothing she couldn't handle.

Andie stood and, hands in the small of her back, arched and stretched stiff muscles. Judging by the sun, she had only a few more minutes if she wanted to hang the herbs in the drying shed before she would have to dress for work.

A mountain bluebird's warbling call glided across the cool air, and Andie spied it among the branches of her massive Scotch pine. Heralds of the rising sun, the Navajo called the little bird. She lifted her face to the sky, content to let the music wash through her.

A string of curses, ripe and inventive, ripped apart the quiet. The bluebird paused for only a moment, then in a flutter of azure wings it soared away.

Well, her tenant was awake, Andie thought, chuckling. And back to his normal irascible self. She gathered her basket and clippers and headed toward the commotion.

Rounding the corner of the barn, she swallowed a laugh at the sight that greeted her. Will was being held hostage by her goat. In full uniform, the lawman glowered at Mr. Whiskers from the cottage steps, watching the goat happily try to munch the driver's door handle on his Jeep. Every time Will attempted to move close enough to climb inside, the animal either kicked out with his hind legs or butted Will with his horns.

She compressed her lips tightly together to contain her mirth, but it bubbled out anyway.

Her tenant turned the full wattage of his glare in her direction. "Call off this damn mangy goat."

"Watch it. You'll hurt his feelings. He can be very sensitive." She grinned.

Will stared at her. "He's a goat."

"But he's very in tune with his inner child. Or kid, I guess you'd say."

"I'm about ready to kick his inner kid from here to Cheyenne if he doesn't quit eating my Jeep."

Andie laughed and held out her free hand. Mr. Whiskers docilely ambled over for her affectionate pat. He lipped the hem of her T-shirt. "Sorry he bothered you. It's just his way of letting you know who's boss." She burrowed her hands in the goat's short, coarse hide. "I usually keep him staked out wherever the grass needs clipping, but lately he's discovered the fun of eating through his leash. Sometimes a goat just needs to run free, I guess."

Will growled deep in his throat, and she couldn't help laughing again. He was surly and humorless, and somehow the combination just made him seem more attractive.

"How's the shoulder?"

"Fine," he said abruptly. He paused and moderated his tone. "Better. The gunk you gave me seemed to help. Thanks."

"You're welcome. When you run out, let me know and I can whip up some more."

"I saw the gardens last night. Did you grow all the things you put in that stuff?"

The reminder of his trip around her property the night before had an unsettling effect on her. She'd always thought of herself as independent and self-sufficient. It was an odd and not completely comfortable revelation for a thirty-two-year-old woman who'd been on her own for years to discover she rather liked the idea of somebody watching out for her.

"Most of it," she answered. "My mom sent me some things I can't cultivate in our short growing season here."

Beyond Will's shoulder Lone Eagle Peak jutted into the sky, harsh and unforgiving and beautiful, its glacial face gleaming in the sun, a harbinger of snows to come. "It's hard to remember, with this heat wave we're having," she added, "but the first hard freeze is just around the corner."

The sheriff followed her gaze to the peak, part of the vast Wind River range. "Quite a place you've got here. One hell of a view."

"I like it." She smiled up at him, wondering what it would take to bring an answering smile to those masculine features, as rough-hewn and frozen as the mountain. "I doubt you'll find anywhere on earth more peaceful."

His jaw worked. "Yeah, well, I'm not looking for peace." He slid into the Jeep.

Unable to help herself, Andie walked over to the vehicle. "What *are* you looking for, Sheriff?"

Will looked away, then back at her, his gray eyes haunted. The grief in them slammed into her stomach like a fist.

"Atonement," he said quietly.

Without another word, he started the Jeep and pulled out of her driveway in a crunch of gravel, leaving her to stare after him, her throat tight and her heart aching.

You don't need this, Andie reminded herself. *You can't be the man's salvation any more than you can jump off the top of Lone Eagle Peak and fly back home.*

Still, she stood watching the empty road for a long time, wondering.

"Beth, sit down before I tie you to the damn chair."

Will's sister pushed a wilted red curl of hair behind her ear and reached into the cupboard over the stove.

"This is *my* kitchen, William Charles Tanner," she said, her voice hollow from inside the cupboard, "and I'm not going to let you boss me around in it."

"And I'm not about to let you wait on me. As soon as Emily and Jace come back from moving the irrigation pipe, she and I will be leaving for our own place. You don't need to fix us dinner, so just take yourself back into that living room and put your feet up. If you had the sense God gave a goose, you'd know that's exactly where you should be."

"Honk honk." She pouted at him but eased herself into one of the chairs around the kitchen table, giving a little sigh of relief even as she grabbed a bowl of string beans, fresh from the garden.

"So how do you like your new landlady?" she asked, her fingers swiftly snapping away.

Will thought of sun-warmed skin and that throaty laugh and long, tanned legs that made him imagine naked heat and sultry nights. His little sister probably didn't want to know he'd barely slept the night before. Every time he'd closed his eyes, Andie McPhee had been there, poking at him, sneaking into his mind with that low laugh and that hidden dimple and those sparkling eyes the color of rain-soaked quaking aspen leaves.

"Fine," he grunted, then reached to help her snap the beans.

"She's turned the Limber Pine into a beautiful little place, hasn't she?" Beth didn't wait for an answer. "You should have seen it when she moved here. The place should have been condemned. No one had lived in it for years, and all the land had been sold off, but she just dug in and poured all she had into fixing it up, then later, opening the preschool."

Beth paused. "She's not had an easy time of it, you know."

Somehow he *had* known. He couldn't explain it rationally. Hell, he didn't even want to try. But something in the way she looked at him whispered of loss and old wounds and shattered dreams.

"No?" he asked his sister, then mentally groaned.

None of your business, Tanner, he reminded himself. *You don't want to know.*

"She doesn't talk about it much, not even to me, and I'm her best friend," Beth said. "I just know she never planned to stay in Whiskey Creek. She was only passing through and had car trouble. By the time Jed down at the gas station had her car going again, she'd bought the Limber Pine, just like that. Paid cash too."

Strange, he thought, his lawman's curiosity piqued.

"She doesn't have family around?"

Beth shook her head. "All she has is her mom in St. Louis. But she's been a good friend to me and to just about everybody else in the valley. We've all sort of adopted her, so be nice to her, or you'll suffer the wrath of the whole county, especially me. You got that, big brother?"

He hadn't exactly been brimming with good manners around the woman, he mused. Seemed like she brought out the worst in him. "I'll consider myself warned."

Beth was still chuckling when Jace and Emily came tromping into the kitchen. Will and Emily left not long afterward, and Emily complained all the way to their new quarters.

It was too hot. Too slow. Too boring.

As much as he hated to admit it, he preferred her grousing to the silent accusations in her eyes—maybe because that was exactly what he saw in his own eyes every time he looked in a mirror.

How could he blame her for being angry with him? Maybe she was just beginning to realize the truth that had burned itself into his cells that terrible day three years ago as he held his dying wife in his arms.

He'd killed Emily's mother.

Oh, he hadn't pulled the trigger, but he might as well have. If it hadn't been for him and his idiotic idealism—his ridiculous, outdated concepts of honor and decency—Sarah would still be alive.

If he'd only taken the payoff when those bastards offered it to him, to keep him away from their paltry racketeering schemes, Sarah would be here, laughing and teasing him as she'd always done.

When Richie Zamora's bribes hadn't worked on him, the crime boss had turned to threats. And Will had laughed. Laughed and told Zamora where he could stick his bribes and his threats and that he damn well better find a good lawyer.

He'd been so arrogant. And naive. Incredibly, stupidly naive.

The next day Sarah, six months pregnant with their son, had died in a hail of gunfire spat from a passing car. And most of him had died with her.

His chance would come, he reminded himself yet again. Zamora was the only one out of the four sons of bitches involved in Sarah's death that he hadn't caught yet. Two would spend the rest of their miserable lives in prison, and the third had died in the same gunfight Will had been wounded in. He would have had Zamora, too, if not for the damn bullet the crime boss had managed to fire into his shoulder.

"When are we going to be there?"

Emily's plaintive voice jerked him out of the past. "It's not far."

As they neared the Limber Pine, Will wrenched his mind away from the thoughts of vengeance that wouldn't do him any good while he was stuck here in Whiskey Creek.

Instead, he thought of his new landlady. He'd never been able to resist a mystery. It was why he'd become a cop in the first place and why he'd earned a reputation as a tenacious investigator.

Why had she settled in this one-stoplight town? What was it that had sent her running here and put those shadows in her eyes? *Not your business, Tanner*, he told himself again.

"Listen, Em, I need you to do something for me," he said suddenly.

"What?" Suspicion coated her voice.

"I need you to stay out of Ms. McPhee's hair while we're living here. She's used to peace and quiet and doesn't need to be disturbed."

"Why would I want to bug some old lady?"

Will frowned, puzzled by the remark, then remembered that Emily had been too busy checking out the preschool to have paid much attention to Andie. "Old lady"? He thought of dewy skin and tempting curves, then gritted his teeth and shunted away the images as guilt washed through him.

"Just try, okay?"

She picked at a hangnail. "Sure. Whatever."

As soon as he'd unlocked the door to their cottage, Emily bounded past him to look at her room, and Will walked into the kitchen wondering what he could possibly make for dinner. He should have had the foresight to go grocery shopping at the little store in Whiskey Creek. Instead, he'd spent the day going over paperwork at the jail and wondering about Andie McPhee.

He scanned the meager contents of the cupboard—a few measly boxes and canned goods Beth had given him the night before. He finally settled on macaroni and cheese and was waiting for the water to boil when several sharp raps indicated a visitor at the back door.

It was his landlady, wearing tattered cutoffs and a bright pink T-shirt and sporting a bulging paper grocery bag. She walked inside and placed the bag on the table before he could say anything.

"I just picked my first sweet corn of the year, and I thought you and Emily might like a few ears for dinner."

Visions of buttery corn on the cob made his mouth water, but Will frowned. "You didn't have to do that."

"I know, but I picked more than I can eat. I don't want to go to all the trouble of freezing it yet, so it's either you guys or the goat."

"It might keep the damn thing away from my Jeep," Will grumbled.

Her laugh rippled over him. Hell, what was it about this woman that so easily tightened his nerves?

He poured the macaroni into the boiling water, and Andie peeked over his shoulder to see what he was making. Intense awareness whipped through him, of her lavender-and-vanilla scent, of her tantalizing heat. *Not your business.*

"Mmmm. Mac and cheese. I lived on the stuff when I was in school." To his relief, she eased away and perched on his kitchen table.

"Where was that?" his innate curiosity compelled him to ask.

"St. Louis. I didn't stray too far from my parents."

She started husking the corn in quick, graceful movements. "I grew up, went away to college, met my husband, and settled down all within a five-mile radius. How's that for an adventurous life?"

Her *husband*? He stared at her, his gaze flying to the fingers of her left hand. No ring. Still, that didn't mean anything.

She caught the direction of his gaze and flushed. "My ex-husband." She concentrated on the corn.

"What about you?" she asked, a blatant attempt to change the subject. "Why did you leave Wyoming? Beth tells me you practically raised her."

"Beth is the undisputed queen of exaggeration."

Andie chuckled. "What makes you say that?"

"I didn't exactly raise her. She was already in high school when our folks died, Dad when a tractor turned over on him, and Mom a year later from pneumonia. I just hung around long enough for her to finish high school, then we both agreed to sell the ranch."

"Was that hard for you, selling the ranch you'd worked all your life? Do you ever regret it?"

"At the time, no. I couldn't wait to leave."

"But now?" she prodded.

He gazed out the window for a minute, then back at her. Her hands had stilled on the corn, and her eyes were soaked with compassion. He didn't want to see it. God knows, he didn't deserve it.

"Yeah. Sometimes."

He'd never felt any particular tie to the land like his father had. He'd wanted adventure, excitement. Something more than birthing calves and riding fence. But if he hadn't been in such a hurry to shed the Wyoming dirt from his boots, he probably would never have become a cop. Never met Sarah. And never lost her.

"Dad, where'd you put my boom box?" Emily demanded from the kitchen doorway.

Then again, he thought, if Sarah hadn't blown into his life, he never would have been given the chance to know the funny, stubborn girl who was his daughter.

"I didn't put it anywhere, Em. It should still be in one of the boxes."

"I've looked everywhere. Are you sure we didn't leave it at Aunt . . . ?" Her voice trailed off as she finally caught sight of Andie, and she stared.

"Hi, Emily," Andie said. "I've been waiting to meet you."

"Who are you?"

Andie ignored the rudeness. "I'm Andie McPhee. I live across the driveway."

The girl studied her out of eyes the same silver gray as her father's. "You don't look old."

She couldn't help laughing at the accusation. "Why, thank you. I think."

"Dad said you were some grumpy old lady who didn't want us to bother you."

Andie glanced at Will and watched, fascinated, as a ruddy tinge spread across his cheekbones.

"I never said you were old," he began.

Before he could say anything more, Emily interrupted. "You're that lady from the little kids' place, with the puppet show thing we saw, aren't you?"

She looked intrigued, and Andie smiled. "I am. You're welcome to come back anytime."

"That stuff's for babies."

Andie shrugged. "Maybe. But if you're interested,

we've got a baby-sitting training program for girls your age. Several girls come in once in a while to read to the children and play with them, just so they can get a feel for being around preschoolers. Who knows, you might even make some new friends before school starts."

"Who wants a bunch of cowboy hicks for friends?"

Emily concentrated on the old linoleum floor, but Andie sensed more than a little loneliness in the girl's tone and in the hunched-up set of her shoulders. She chanced a look at Will and saw bleak frustration in his eyes as he studied his daughter. *Stay out of it*, she reminded herself sternly.

Still, she smiled one more time at Emily. "If you change your mind, let me know. We don't expect the girls to work for free and we'll pay you for the time you spend at the school. Think about it, okay?"

"Okay," Emily mumbled. She left in a cloud of hair spray and attitude.

"I swear, I never said you were old," Will said with such chagrin in his voice that Andie laughed.

To her shock, he actually smiled back, and for a moment it was all she could do to remember to breathe. The man was gorgeous. A simple smile transformed those craggy features into somebody warm and friendly. Sexy and intriguing and masculine.

A slow warmth uncurled in her stomach as she watched him standing there, a lock of brown hair dipping into his eyes and his smile melting his reserve.

She took a shaky breath and tugged down the husk on the last ear of corn, then pushed herself away from the table.

"I need to get back. Um, enjoy the corn."

She left in a hurry, the screen door slamming shut behind her.

Andie fluffed a pillow and squinted at her alarm clock. One A.M., the blasted thing blared in glowing red numbers, and here she was still wide awake.

The room, with its graceful old furniture and flowery wallpaper, seemed stifling. Overpowering.

A little breeze, moist and cool, danced in through the open window and puffed into the lace curtains, sending them billowing like the sails of a ship. Andie suddenly craved the feel of that breeze. She slipped from her bed and peered out the window. A storm lurked out there; she could feel it crackling in the air. Probably a good, pounding August thunderstorm.

That's what was keeping her up, she told herself, the storm and all those negative ions floating around. *Liar*, a voice whispered deep inside, and she had to acknowledge that, as usual, the know-it-all voice was right. What was keeping her edgy and awake had nothing to do with any storm and everything to do with a wounded, angry sheriff with hot, haunted eyes and a dangerous smile.

Well, no use moping around in here. She wasn't going to sleep any time soon, so she might as well go out and enjoy the night. Without bothering to turn on the light, she donned a robe over her nightgown and went downstairs, stepping out the front door onto the broad porch.

The porch that wrapped all the way around the old house was one of the reasons she'd bought the ranch. A silly reason for such a significant life change, she'd often thought. But the first time she saw the ranch, she'd immediately envisioned sitting there on a summer night while a storm percolated just out of view.

She sat on the porch swing, pulling her bare feet up under her. Fred, the tiger-striped tom with the torn ear and fifteen pounds of bad mood, pounced onto her lap for affection. Not to be outdone, Wilma—his long-suffering mate—joined him, and soon their combined purring vibrated through the night.

Andie smiled and inhaled air rich with the promise of moisture and the heavy perfume of sweet peas and the wild roses that climbed the lattice around the porch.

The wind picked up, tossing the tendrils of the weeping willow into wild contortions. She could hear the storm gathering force in the mountains, and as she stroked the cats, she imagined the violence there, the pounding rains, the low drum roll of thunder.

Where were the dogs? she wondered. Usually a good rousing thunderstorm set them to howling, or at least scratching on the door looking for cover. She often gave in and let them sleep inside, but tonight they were nowhere in sight.

As if in answer to her thoughts, lightning suddenly jagged across the sky, and she saw both big yellow Labs heading around the corner of the barn at a full run toward her.

She grinned as she watched them streak across the yard, until she saw the figure step out behind them. Her heartbeat quickened and her mouth suddenly felt dry. Will Tanner followed the dogs around the barn, and she knew instantly when he spied her. His strong, purposeful stride faltered and he stopped.

"I thought I was alone out here with the storm," she called.

He walked to the steps of the porch, then stood there looking as dark and foreboding as the clouds that churned overhead.

"I couldn't sleep," he said.

"Neither could I."

The rain began spitting from the clouds in huge drops, and another rumble of thunder shook the night.

"You're going to be soaked to the skin in a minute if you stay there," she warned, curling her fingers into the fur on one of the dogs' back. "Why don't you come sit down and enjoy the storm where it's warm and dry?"

She thought he would refuse, that he would turn and march back across the driveway to his own place. But he just shrugged, climbed the steps, and settled into the spacious old rocker beside her.

FOUR

With a push of her foot, Andie set the porch swing swaying again, its chains rattling. The sound, combined with the slow creak of Will's rocker, set a gentle backbeat to the storm whipping around them.

It was oddly intimate, she thought, sitting comfortable and dry on the porch while the weather spewed its fury just a few feet away. The hard rain slanting down created a shimmery curtain of sorts, a wall of privacy between them and the rest of the world.

They sat in silence for several minutes while the storm picked up in intensity. She could sense Will relaxing, in contrast to the storm, settling into the old chair as if it had been years since he'd sat down. Through the watery moonlight she saw him lean his head back and close his eyes, and she couldn't hide her pleased smile.

"That's a wonderful smell, isn't it?" she said softly. "The rain soaking into the earth. Like hope and birth. Life."

He inhaled deeply. "A rainstorm smells different

here in the mountains than the desert. Softer somehow. In Phoenix there's always an edge of desperation
to it, like each drop is going to be the last."

One of the dogs stuck its nose in Will's lap, and he
opened his eyes and scratched its ears absently. The
gentleness there startled her. He was a man of contra-
dictions: kind one moment, gruff the next; affectionate
with the dogs, abrupt with her. She didn't quite know
how to deal with him.

"I watched you last night," she said, "walking
around out here to check the place out."

His mouth twisted in a self-mocking grimace.
"Sorry. Old habit, I guess. I've been in too many situa-
tions where a little knowledge of my surroundings
made the difference between taking a bullet and walking away."

"I didn't mind. It was kind of . . . comforting."

He shot her an inscrutable look. "This is a pretty
isolated spot for a woman on her own."

She shrugged. "It's only three miles into town and
three more the other way to the Bar W."

"Well, I couldn't find one single sign that you've
taken any kind of security precautions. Don't you realize you'd have no way of calling for help if anything
happened out here? I could do anything I wanted with
you right now and nobody would ever hear a damn
thing."

With any other man she might have felt threatened
by the ominous statement, even though he delivered it
in a cool, matter-of-fact tone. But somehow Andie
knew he would never pose a physical danger to her,
despite the ease with which he sent her emotions into
turmoil.

"I don't scare easily, Sheriff."

He snorted. "That's about the stupidest thing I've heard you say. You let down your guard even for a second, and you can be damn sure somebody's going to take advantage of you."

"Sounds like a pretty miserable way to experience life, if you ask me," she said mildly. "I'd rather have a little faith in other people."

"So would I," he said in a clipped voice. "And I'd rather believe in Santa Claus and the Tooth Fairy too."

A spear of lightning illuminated his face, and she saw a grim tightness around his mouth, shadows in his gray wolf eyes. Andie suddenly realized he had seen things in his life as a police officer, things she could never even imagine. It was no wonder he had so few illusions about human nature and, like those desert storms, so little softness left in him.

Thunder, harsh and close, plowed through the night, rattling the windows on the old farmhouse. Andie shivered.

"You're cold," he said. "Maybe you ought to go inside."

"Not yet." She summoned a smile. "A good summer storm is too precious to waste watching from the inside. In another few months that will be snow out there, and I'll have more time indoors than I can stand. Then I can remember tonight, with the rain stirring up the dirt and the wind blowing fresh and clean from the mountains."

"How do you manage here in the winter? Unless it's changed since I lived in the state, Wyoming in January is a whole lot of nasty."

She chuckled. "It's not that bad. Neighbors take care of each other out here. That's one of the reasons I love it so much. By the end of October, Sam Wyatt down the road always brings me plenty of firewood, and Jace comes by with his tractor after every big storm to dig me out."

"What brought you out here, anyway, to Whiskey Creek? To such an isolated place?"

Fred bristled as her hands tensed in his fur, and Andie forced herself to relax. Would there ever come a time when she could remember the past without this awful regret, the terrible sense of failure?

She picked her words carefully. "I had just been through a rough divorce."

"Is there any other kind?"

"Good point." She gave a dry laugh. "I'm afraid I don't have much patience any more for those divorced couples who say they had an amicable parting. They're just better at swallowing their feelings than the rest of us. And probably have more ulcers as a result."

She stared out into the night. "I was wrung out already from some—some physical problems." Andie almost laughed again at the severe understatement. "I knew our marriage was on the brink of disintegrating. It had been that way for a long time, so I guess it shouldn't have shocked me so much when it crumbled away. Then two days after the divorce was final my father died suddenly."

Will made a sympathetic sound, and she shivered again. She'd always feared her divorce had somehow precipitated her father's massive heart attack. Both her parents had been deeply disappointed when her marriage didn't survive.

"It was more than I could handle emotionally," she said quietly. "The day after my father's funeral I packed the car and hit the road. I'd planned to visit an old high-school friend in the Seattle area, but I landed in Whiskey Creek and discovered this is where I wanted to stay."

There was more, much more, she thought. Her deeply rooted shame that she hadn't been strong enough to stay and fight for a marriage that had been shaky from the very beginning, her bitter disappointment at Peter for being so weak and ineffectual against his parents' constant haranguing, the lingering heartache at leaving so much behind.

Despite it all, she loved the life she'd carved out for herself. The ranch and the school gave her a satisfaction she'd never found anywhere else, and she'd discovered a profound and enduring love for the land, for the quicksilver seasons and the harsh beauty, for the contrasts and the wildness.

Most of all, she'd come to love the people, with their work-hardened hands and their weather-etched faces, as if they were her own family. They had drawn her inside their world, as if she'd lived there forever.

"You know," she added, "your sister's largely to blame for turning what was supposed to be a quick detour into a permanent home."

"Why's that?"

"My marriage was over, my life was in shambles, and even my car decided to betray me by breaking down just outside of town. I was sitting over at R.J.'s Café, basically having a 'poor me' pity party while I waited for the mechanic to figure out what was wrong with the car. Well, Beth walked into the café, spotted me brooding in the corner, and plopped herself down in the booth."

Andie smiled at the memory. "She told me that since she knew every single soul in the county, she knew I couldn't possibly be a local. She'd stopped by because she felt it was her civic duty to warn me, if I cared at all about the lining of my stomach, not to try R.J.'s chicken-fried steak."

A chuckle rasped out of him. "Sounds like Beth."

"I figured a town that cared so much for its visitors' health couldn't be all bad. The next day I took a long walk while I was waiting for my car to be fixed and saw a for-sale sign outside the Limber Pine. The rest, as they say, is history."

It had been more spite than anything, she had to admit, a quick way to spend the obscene amount of alimony she'd been granted, alimony she hadn't asked for or wanted. The guilt money Peter had insisted on giving her, his salve to his conscience for what he saw as discarding damaged property.

Andie supposed she'd subconsciously spent the money so wildly and impulsively as her last rebellion, something the oh-so-correct Peter and his civilized parents would find completely incomprehensible. It seemed petty and childish now, but then she'd been young and wounded and had wanted to strike back.

Despite her small-minded motives, settling in Whiskey Creek had been the best thing possible for her, had given her life direction. Had brought her dear friends who had welcomed her into their lives.

"You know," she said, "I'd never had a friend like Beth before. She's the most caring person I've ever met. You did a good job with her."

He laughed, again with that self-mocking edge. "I can't take credit for the way my little sister turned out."

"You helped raise her, didn't you? You had to have done something right."

"I'm sure not having much luck with Emily." He spoke quietly, his words edged with a resigned failure she recognized only too well.

"Problems?"

He stopped rocking and was silent for a long time. "I can't reach her anymore," he finally said. "It's like she changed overnight from a little girl to somebody I don't know. I have no clue what she wants or what she needs, and she won't tell me."

"It's a hard age for a girl. If she knew herself what was wrong, she'd probably tell you, Will."

"Things were going okay, I thought. We were managing. I wasn't home much, I'll admit it, but she seemed happy enough."

Peering through the dark, Andie could see his hands were clenched on the arms of the rocker.

"Then about three months ago, I was stupid enough to get myself shot, and it seemed like I woke up in the hospital to a different kid. It's like she's angry about something, but I can't get her to tell me what it is. Hell, she barely even talks to me."

He sighed. "All year long she had good grades, then in the spring she just quit doing her homework and started hanging out with a bunch of older kids. Skipping school. Lying about things. Hell, she's only eleven years old, and I caught her trying to sneak out one night. I thought it might be her new friends, that they were just a bad influence on her. I told myself if I could just get her away from them for a while, she'd settle back down."

"Has it worked?"

"Not that I've seen. Now she's even angrier at me for dragging her here to what she considers the end of the world. She barely has a civil word for me."

"Maybe you could find something to do with her while you're here, like horseback riding. It seems like just about every girl her age is crazy about horses. Jace would probably lend you a gentle saddle horse while you're here. She's welcome to keep it in the pasture."

Will frowned. "I don't know. I honestly don't know her anymore. What the hell kind of a parent am I when I have no idea what she likes?"

"Don't be so hard on yourself, Will. As far as I know, there are no hard and fast rules about what makes a good parent other than giving your child unconditional love. And maybe don't feed them mac and cheese for every meal," she teased.

He glanced at her. "It helps to talk about it with someone. Thanks for listening."

"Anytime," she said, and meant it. They sat quietly for several more minutes, and she thought how nice it was to have someone to talk to. She hadn't even realized how much she'd missed this, having another person to share her thoughts with.

While she swayed, she gradually became aware that the storm was fading. The pyrotechnics slowed and then stopped completely until there was only the rain, a hushed sigh in the darkness.

Content to let the now-gentle night sounds wash through her, she leaned her head back against the hard slats of the porch swing and closed her eyes. Her wide yawn seemed to come out of nowhere. She covered her mouth, but Will must have seen it. In one lithe motion, he rose to his feet.

"I guess that's my cue to go."

"I'm sorry, Will." She could feel herself flushing. "It's just been a long week and I'm afraid it's beginning to catch up with me."

"Well, thanks for sharing the storm with me. I, uh, I enjoyed it."

Maybe it was because he stumbled over the words, as if he had found few things to enjoy recently, but Andie instinctively reached a hand out and touched his arm, intending to offer comfort.

He flexed his bicep at the contact, and she felt the corded muscle there, the heat and the strength. As it had the day before in his kitchen when they touched, electricity crackled between them, more potent than any summer thunderstorm, and she jerked her hand away as if she'd touched a live wire.

"You're—you're welcome," she whispered.

He gave her a long, searching look, then turned and walked out into the rain.

"Come on, Andie. Open up," Will muttered. He glanced at his watch and swore under his breath. He had one hell of a nerve knocking on her door at two A.M. on a Friday night, but he didn't have too many other options. If he didn't hustle his butt over to the Stockman, he was going to have more trouble than just a stupid bar fight to deal with, judging by his deputy's near-hysterical phone call a few minutes before.

"You gotta come, Sheriff," Joey Whitehorse had

shouted into the phone. "The way they're going, somebody's gonna get killed."

It was a pretty sorry situation when his deputies couldn't handle a lousy bar fight. No wonder Hank hadn't wanted to leave any of them in charge.

He knocked again impatiently, and the door swung open. Andie stood there, her dark hair tousled, wearing another one of those plain white cotton nightgowns and a matching robe like she'd had on the other night. His gut clenched.

"Will! What's wrong? Is it Beth?" The lingering sleep disappeared from her eyes.

"No. Bunch of drunk cowboys are fighting it out down at the Stockman, and Joey called for backup. Problem is, Beth and Jace stayed over in Jackson for her doctor's appointment, and I don't know what to do with Emily."

"I'll stay with her," Andie said immediately.

"I was hoping you'd say that." He grimaced. He didn't deserve her help the way he'd been avoiding her all week, ever since they'd shared the storm together.

Something had happened between them that night, some indefinable softening and settling in their relationship. He could feel both her fresh exuberance and quiet compassion tugging at him. At odd times during the day he found himself staring off into space thinking about her, the way her eyes lit up with an inner fire when she talked about something she cared about, how her smile seemed to sneak out from nowhere.

Nearly every night he'd seen her working in the garden or feeding the animals or just sitting on the porch swing, swaying gently in the evening breeze.

And nearly every night he had to battle a powerful urge to go to her, to share with her some little thing that had happened that day. About Mrs. Rossetti's stolen laundry. About old Seth Checkett's ornery bull he'd helped corral after it went on a wild rampage through town. About the two little towheaded boys who stopped at the jail every day around noon, just to "chew the fat"—as they called it—with the sheriff.

He could feel the easy pace of the town and the woman who seemed to fit in so well casting a charming, soothing spell on him. And he was fighting it with every ounce of strength he had left. He couldn't afford to let her or the town slip under his skin any more than they'd already done, didn't dare let down his guard.

"I'm happy to do it," she answered now. Barefoot, she picked her way across the driveway toward the cottage. He followed her, trying like hell not to notice the way her white robe swirled around her long legs or the way her dark hair caught the moonbeams.

"I could probably leave her alone—she's nearly twelve, after all," Will said when they reached the kitchen door. "But she . . . lately she's been having these nightmares. She used to get them after her mother died, and they came back just a month or so ago. I'd hate for her to have one and wake up with no one there."

"Don't worry about it. Just be careful, Will, okay?" In that damn physical way of hers, she reached out a hand to touch his arm, and both of them froze.

As had happened a week ago, he felt his breath catch, felt the rapid pulse of blood spilling through his body like water from a dam, and he cursed his unwilling response to her.

She was beautiful, even just roused from sleep. Or maybe especially just roused from sleep. Without any artificial enhancement, she looked fresh and appealing, a rosy hue underlying her sun-kissed skin. But what wrenched at him most had nothing to do with the adorable freckles on her nose or the lush softness of her lips.

It was the concern that darkened the startling green of her eyes. How long had it been since he'd had anybody to worry about him? He didn't like it, he told himself. Didn't need it. But the fact that she cared about his safety warmed some place cold and dark deep inside him.

Involuntarily, he clenched his fist, flexing his muscle, and her hand immediately lifted from his arm. He was glad, he told himself fiercely, and cleared his throat. "I shouldn't be gone longer than an hour or so."

He shoved on the tan Stetson that came with his Whiskey Creek uniform and walked out, swearing at himself for letting her get to him once again.

Andie tried to sleep after Will left, but she was too aware of him here in the cottage. After he packed away his aching soul and his funny, defiant daughter and left Whiskey Creek for good, would she ever be able to walk into the place without seeing him there, without smelling that subtle pine-and-cedar scent that clung to him? She knew she'd never be able to enjoy another summer storm without thinking of sitting on the porch swing while he rocked beside her, in peaceful contrast to the violence of the night.

Her last thought before drifting into sleep was that she would have to guard her heart well. She'd worked too hard to find happiness again to let a wounded warrior like Will Tanner leave her bruised and broken when he decided to march on.

She didn't know how long she'd been asleep when a hushed cry jerked her upright on the couch, her heart pounding. Emily! She must be having one of those nightmares Will had warned her about.

Not wanting to scare the girl, Andie eased quietly into her room. Compassion and tenderness welled up inside her at the distressed sounds coming from Will's daughter. Anguished murmurs sounded in her throat, and she tossed her head restlessly on the pillow.

Andie knelt beside the bed and laid her hand on Emily's skinny arm.

"Dad, where are you?" the girl whispered, and Andie gently squeezed her arm.

"Shhh. Emily. It's only a dream, sweetheart."

"Don't leave me, Daddy. Don't leave. Please. *Please.*"

She didn't awaken, but Andie's presence seemed to help her calm down. After a few more minutes of shifting on the bed, her breathing slowed and she settled into a deeper stage of sleep, her features again relaxed.

It gave Andie time to look at her. In sleep, Emily lost her air of belligerence, looking innocent and sweet instead.

Her first child would have been four years younger than Emily.

The thought sneaked up on her, and Andie had to concentrate to steady her breathing against the sudden, piercing pain. It had been a boy, the doctor had told her in his clinical, but not unkind, voice. A perfect little boy who had never had a chance at life.

With the ease of long practice, Andie forced her thoughts away. She smoothed Emily's hair back from her sticky forehead until she had her own breathing—and her thoughts—carefully under control.

Poor thing, she thought, touching Emily's cheek. To lose her mother in such a violent way had to have been devastating. And then to nearly lose her father must have terrified her.

Maybe that was why her nightmares had reemerged. It seemed likely, especially since she'd called out for her father not to leave. Maybe Will's gunshot wounds had revived the terrible loss of her mother. It could also explain why the girl had changed in the last few months into a wild rebel, searching for attention from her distant, preoccupied father.

She felt a sudden rush of anger at Will. Was he so consumed with his own grief over the death of his wife that he had forgotten his child was grieving too? Still, it wasn't any of her business, was it? She was just the landlady, and he was just the stubborn, ornery man she couldn't keep out of her thoughts.

When she was sure Emily had settled down again, Andie rose. She knew she was too keyed up now to sleep, so she walked back to her house for the mystery she'd left on her nightstand, then returned to the cottage to curl up with it on the couch.

She was still there two hours later when she heard Will's Jeep pull up outside. She walked to the kitchen to greet him, and an involuntary gasp escaped her when he opened the door.

"What on earth happened to you?"

He gave a sheepish half smile, then winced as the motion jostled the deep red bruise ringing one eye. "You ought to see the other guy. 'Course, you'd have to go down to the jail to do it."

"That'll teach him not to mess with the sheriff," she teased. "We frown on that around here. Lock him up and throw away the key, that's what you should do."

"Well, he'll only be down there for a few more hours. At least that's when his shift ends."

Andie burst out laughing, then stopped so she didn't wake Emily. "You were slugged by your own deputy?"

"Yeah." Will wore a disgruntled frown.

"Which one, Joey or Wade?"

"Whitehorse."

"I didn't know Joey had it in him."

"Neither did he." Will rolled his eyes, then winced at the motion. "I nearly had things settled down, and some drunk idiot took a swing at him. Joe punched back, and I somehow managed to step into the way. Everybody else joined in, and it took us another twenty minutes to clear out the damn place."

"Here. Let me take a look at it." She reached on tiptoe and cupped his chin to turn his head for a better view.

Time seemed to grind to a jerky stop.

Too late she realized how close she was standing to him, her breasts pushed against his chest, the length of her body resting on his. She could feel the heat of him, feel the leashed power in his hard muscles, feel the steady rhythm of his heartbeat. Her own heartbeat seemed to pick up a pace as a seductive warmth un-coiled deep inside her.

He must not have shaved before leaving earlier, she mused, because his skin against her fingers felt rough and stubbled. Erotic and male. Her breath snagged in her throat and her gaze locked with his. She watched, frozen, barely breathing, as naked desire dilated his pupils, darkening the silver to a cloudy gray.

He whispered an oath even as his arms imprisoned her, as his mouth consumed hers. That summer storm came to mind again, sizzling energy, pounding, vio-lent, churning. At first she was too surprised to do more than stand there. Then she was too stunned by the heat zinging through her body, by the hunger that seemed to come out of nowhere.

Her eyes slid shut and she forgot to breathe, forgot to think, forgot everything but the dark and wild won-der of it. How long had it been since she'd felt so alive, so wonderfully, terribly alive?

His mouth danced against hers again and again, pulling at her, tugging at her soul. Somehow, without realizing it, she'd entwined her arms around him and she clutched at his back, pulling him closer. Muscles taut, he pressed her against the kitchen counter, his hands buried in her hair, and she nearly cried out at the need surging through her.

She knew the world continued spinning because she had vague awareness of life outside the circle of their bodies. The whir of the refrigerator. The counter gouging into her back. The ticking of a clock somewhere in the house.

Nothing else mattered, though. The only thing

with meaning was Will. His mouth on hers, slick and hot and demanding. His body, hard and urgent. The cedar tang of his skin, meshed with the faint, slightly wicked echoes of liquor and tobacco from the Stockman.

Andie heard a soft moan of arousal and realized with some surprise it came from her own throat. Will, as if jerked back to his senses by the sound, suddenly stiffened.

His arms slid away and he stared at her. "I don't want this," he growled, backing away. "I don't want you. I can't."

His words pierced through the cotton-soft haze of desire enveloping her, ripping into her like a jagged blade.

I don't want you. So familiar. So cruelly familiar. She took a shuddering breath while shame and hurt burned through her.

Hands shaking, Andie turned and opened the freezer door. The frigid air puffing out did absolutely nothing to cool her fevered skin, her scorched emotions, and she closed her eyes for a moment, trying to regain control while anger and desire and old pain warred within her.

I don't want you.

It shouldn't hurt so much, not after five years. First Peter, now Will.

I can't want you. You understand, don't you, Andie?

She didn't. She never would.

Very carefully, she removed some ice cubes, closed the freezer door, and reached for the dish towel hooked over the oven door to wrap the ice in. "If you don't want that eye to be swollen shut in the morning, you'd better put this on it." She was immensely proud of herself that the words came out as cool as the ice she held in her hands.

"You're right." Will stood watching her warily, as if he expected her to dump the pack, ice and all, on his head.

She was tempted to, but it would have taken more energy than she could summon right then. Instead, she handed the towel to him without touching him and headed for the door.

His voice, rough and low, made her falter for a moment. "I'm sorry, Andie."

She turned back. Even with one Technicolor eye and his hair mussed from her fingers, he was gorgeous. Beautifully, ruggedly male, with his sculpted features and that shock of thick, auburn-streaked brown hair.

She wanted to step right back into his arms, she realized with shock. How could she possibly be so weak, so completely and utterly powerless? Disgusted with herself, she stiffened her spine and continued walking.

The phone was ringing when she opened the door to the ranch house. It was probably her friendly breather, she thought, and decided to ignore the strident ringing. She couldn't handle it. Not tonight.

Tonight she would just climb into her bed and lie there alone and try to forget. To block from her mind the taste of him, the feel of his heat under her fingertips, the way their bodies meshed together as perfectly as the mountains and sky outside her window.

And all the reasons he would never want her.

FIVE

Will rotated his bad shoulder as he opened the door to the sheriff's office. It seemed a little better. Still not quite up to his old abilities, but he could move it with more flexibility, and it seemed to be regaining the strength Zamora's bullet had shattered.

It must be all this clean living, he thought, and surprised himself with a rusty chuckle. He'd learned in the past month that despite its wild and woolly name, Whiskey Creek didn't offer much in the way of vices.

The reason he felt so good surely couldn't have anything to do with that ointment his landlady had given him. Or with the odd, sparkling emotions she sent twisting through him, could it?

He hadn't seen Andie since their heated embrace of nearly a week before—hadn't wanted to see her. In fact, he'd done all he could to avoid her, working long shifts and spending most of his free hours at the Bar W helping Jace put his hay in for the winter.

Hell, he'd even taken her advice and eased his old body onto one of the Bar W horses and gone out with

Emily on a couple of rides, for all the good it had done him.

No matter how hard he worked, though, no matter how far he rode, he hadn't been able to escape her. The memory of her lips on his, warm and welcoming and *alive*, of the coming-home feeling of being in her arms, always hovered on the fringes of his mind, waiting for him to relax his guard.

As if his thoughts had conjured her, he heard a familiar low laugh. It tightened his gut, and his heartbeat picked up a pace. He followed the irresistibly compelling sound into the jail office and found Andie perched on a desk, laughing at something one of his deputies had said. Both Joe Whitehorse and Wade Jenkins, set for their shift change, were hovering around her like bees on honeysuckle.

His good mood disappeared. "Nice to see you two have so much damn time on your hands," he said.

If he hadn't been fighting a sensation that felt suspiciously like jealousy, he would have laughed at the way his two deputies jumped to attention. He had no idea they viewed him as such an ogre.

"Sheriff Tanner. Sir," Joe began. "Andie was just, uh . . . we were just . . ."

Will took pity on him. The kid was green, but he had a dedication to the job that Will envied. Once, a long time ago, he'd had his share of that same enthusiasm.

"I just got a call on my C-phone," he said to the deputies, "about some kids spray-painting something on a grain silo down at the Peterson place. Why don't you two go check it out."

"Both of us?"

"Either of you got a problem with that?" He stared the two men down.

"No. No, sir." They both grabbed their hats from the rack and rushed out the door, nearly knocking each other over in their haste to escape. He sighed and turned back to Andie.

Of course, she had that smile on her face, the one that always made him fear she was secretly laughing at him.

"Your eye looks good, Sheriff. Not much swelling and only a bit of color."

The last time she'd looked at his eye, she'd stepped closer for a better view, he remembered, and he'd ended up crushing her against the counter. A vision of her wrapped around him in his kitchen, her skin soft and seductive, her mouth sweet and hot, made his stomach clench with need. Hungry, aching need. He frowned and forced it away.

"What can I do for you, Ms. McPhee?" he asked curtly.

She studied him for a moment, then straightened off his desk and slid into a chair, folding her hands demurely in front of her. "I want you to arrest somebody."

"You have somebody in mind, or would just anybody do?"

She frowned. "Somebody in particular. A rancher named Tom Jessop."

"Jessop? I don't believe I've had the pleasure of meeting him."

"Lucky for you," she muttered.

Will took a seat behind the desk and pulled out a notepad, more grateful than he cared to admit that she'd given him a diversion from his wayward thoughts. "What'd the poor guy do? Give you a bad load of manure?"

"It's more like what he didn't do."

"Meaning?"

She pursed her lips. "How much do you know about the migrant laborers around here?"

"Not much. Most of them don't cause any trouble, so I haven't had much to do with them. Why?" He was instantly alert. "Has one of them been bothering you?"

"No," she assured him. "Not at all. It's nothing like that."

"What's the problem, then?"

"I work with many of their children at the pre-school. We have a grant through the Migrant Head Start program, and you'd be surprised how much information filters through there. I know quite a bit about what goes on at some of the bigger ranches, and most of the ranchers treat their workers decently enough."

"But not Jessop?" It was the logical guess.

Andie's eyes blazed with anger. "Jessop is the worst. He has six families living at the Rocking J this time of year to help him with the harvest and some fruit orchards he has. He works them twelve to eighteen hours a day without a break. I'm surprised nobody's been killed. Do you know how dangerous farm work can be, especially for an exhausted worker?"

For an instant, Will thought of his father, trapped and bleeding to death under a tractor for hours until Will came home and found him out in the far pasture.

"Yeah, I know," he said tersely.

Compassion and understanding softened her features. "I'm sorry, Will. Of course you do." She paused. "Well, Jessop has about twenty people—many of them children—living in one-room shacks without electricity or running water."

"If they're so miserable, why don't they leave?"

"To go where? There aren't exactly a surplus of jobs in these parts, and it takes money to move on. Jessop makes sure they don't have the funds to leave until after the harvest."

Will frowned as her words stirred up an old enthusiasm for the job—the desire to correct injustice, to make things right. It was one of the things that had drawn him to police work and was also the very thing he had come to despise.

"What about social service agencies? Can't they step in?"

"These people don't want handouts. They just want a decent job and a decent place to live in."

Something of his cynicism must have shown on his face, because she scowled at him.

"You don't believe me, do you?"

"I didn't say that, Andie."

"You didn't have to say it."

"Look, I'll check it out, go to the Rocking J and ask some questions. That's about the best I can do at this point."

"They won't talk to you," she predicted. "They see a uniform and get ready to bolt. Even though most of them have workers' visas, they don't like to take any chances with the authorities."

"Just what is it you expect me to do, then?"

Her hands twisted in her lap. It was the first time

he'd ever seen her anything less than completely self-assured. *Except when her body was molded against him and her mouth was singing an erotic harmony with his.* He found himself staring at that mouth, at the way her full bottom lip jutted out slightly, at the tiny beauty mark almost hidden in the fold where her lips met. When he realized the direction his thoughts had taken, he cursed inwardly and dragged his attention back to the case. "How can I investigate if I can't even see for myself what's going on?"

"I—I could go with you," she said. "They trust me and they'd talk to me about it."

Hell no! He started to refuse. How could he possibly spend more time with her without risking a repeat of their passion from the week before? He wanted her, craved the feel of her with a fierce, urgent ache. And he hated himself for the weakness.

Still, he thought, for the next two months he was the law in Whiskey Creek, and he'd sworn to do his best to protect the people in his jurisdiction. If Jessop's place was as bad as she said, Will would have to do something about it. He couldn't let the fact that he was unable to control his reaction to her stand in the way.

"Can you leave now?" he finally asked.

She nodded and stood up. "I'm ready. I'll warn you, though. Tom and I have already gone a few rounds on this. He promised Hank earlier this summer he'd clean the place up, but I went out yesterday and not one single thing has been done."

"Maybe he figures with Hank laid up nobody will bother him about it."

"Well, I plan to go on bothering him until he

makes some changes. If Tom sees you with me, he probably won't let you on his land. He thinks I'm nothing but a troublemaker."

On that, at least, he and Jessop would agree, Will thought. She was nothing *but* trouble, wrapped up in one hell of a package.

The work camp was everything Andie had said and worse. The stench of neglect hung heavily over the motley collection of shanties that looked as if they'd blow over in a stiff wind. Built of what appeared to be leftover barn planks, plywood, and anything else handy, the shacks had no glass covering the few windows, just tacked-up sheets of plastic. A dilapidated outhouse behind the structures was the only evidence of plumbing he could see.

Will watched Andie pick up a little girl of about three who sported a bright blue cast on her arm. The child spoke in quick, high-pitched Spanish to Andie, who must have understood because she obligingly kissed the cast the girl thrust at her before brushing her lips over the child's dirty cheek and setting her down.

A tired-looking woman stood in the doorway of one shack, wearing jeans and a T-shirt and watching them cautiously. She must have recognized Andie, because her features relaxed and she lifted a hand in greeting.

Andie walked over to her and spoke rapidly in Spanish. With his limited command of the language, Will picked up the words *police* and *help*, but most of it was a blur. Whatever she'd said must have worked, though. The woman gave him a wide smile and gestured at the doorway, pushing back a beat-up door hanging crookedly on its hinges.

He followed the woman inside and had to catch his breath at the propane smell oozing from a camp stove in one corner. He spied a mattress covered with sleeping bags and a rickety table set for dinner, with three little faces around it beaming at him. Despite its primitive exterior, the inside of the shack was clean, and he could tell the woman had done all she could to make it homey.

When the other children saw Andie, they slid out of their chairs and raced to her. Will watched while she laughed and hugged each one.

"How long have they been here?" he asked.

Andie spoke to the woman, then turned back to him. "Juana says a month this time. They were here last year for most of the summer, and her husband Frederico worked for another outfit farther south, but nobody else in the area needed extra help this year, so they're stuck with Jessop."

Another rapid exchange followed, then the woman headed for the cook stove.

"Their youngest, little Teresa there," Andie went on, "fell out of a tree and broke her arm just after they arrived. Jessop won't give them what they've earned, and they don't want to move on until their debt to Doc Matthews at the clinic is paid."

The woman handed each of her children a bowl of food, then filled another one and presented it to Will. He nearly refused, but Andie gave a subtle shake of her head, so he smiled and took it.

"*Gracias*," he said. He took a taste of the rice dish, which turned out to be surprisingly good.

The woman smiled and said something to Andie. To his surprise, Andie blushed and replied, shaking her head vigorously while refusing to look at him.

"What did she say?" Will asked, curious despite himself.

She glanced at him, her green eyes shimmering with mingled laughter and embarrassment. "She said my man looks strong and handsome when he smiles. Of course I told her you weren't 'my man,' but for some reason she didn't believe me."

He felt heat soak his own cheeks and spent the rest of their time in the little shanty trying fiercely to keep his expression smile free.

With Andie translating, Will asked the woman several more questions, then took a quick tour of the other workers' housing. It wasn't until they had left Jessop's property and were heading back to Whiskey Creek that he and Andie had a chance to speak about anything other than the camp.

"You seem like you have a good command of Spanish," he said. "Where did you pick it up?"

"My mother is from Guatemala." She said the words with a slightly belligerent lift of her chin. "She and my grandparents migrated here when she was young, looking for a better life. Maybe that's why I'm so passionate about this."

"Andie McPhee doesn't sound very Hispanic."

She laughed, and he clenched his fingers on the steering wheel as the sultry sound slid through him.

"Try Andrea Milagros de Valdez McPhee. It was quite a mouthful when I was a kid. I guess that's what

happens when you have an Irish father and a Guate-
malan mother."

"Milagros. Miracles. Isn't that the translation?"

A dusky rose tinted the curve of her cheekbones.
"My parents were older when they had me. My
mother was nearly forty-three. They were both college professors. Mama's a botanist and Dad taught lit-
erature. To them, I was a miracle, I guess," she
finished, just as they pulled up in front of the rock
building that housed the jail and sheriff's office.

Andie opened her door as if she couldn't wait to
escape. "So when are you going to go arrest Jessop?"
she asked, one foot on the ground.

"I'm not," he said bluntly.

"You're not?" She climbed back in and stared at
him across the width of the vehicle. "What do you
mean, you're not? You just saw what conditions he's
making them live under there. How can you simply
walk away from that and do nothing?"

"I never said I wasn't going to do anything, Andie.
And I'm not going to walk away. I just said I wasn't
going to arrest him. This is a misdemeanor offense at
best, and even then I doubt I can bring charges until I
have health and building inspectors down from
Pinedale to check it out."

"In the meantime, the workers are living in absolutely deplorable conditions and there's not one single
thing they can do about it."

"I'm sorry, Andie. I'll work as fast as I can. But this
is not the Wild West anymore. I have to work through
channels. I can't just ride in like I'm Marshal Dillon or
something and haul Jessop off to jail."

"Of course not." Her voice held contempt and

weary resignation. "They're only migrant workers, after all. They don't need to have a decent place to live. Why don't they just go back to their own country where they belong and leave the good jobs that pay ten dollars a day for the rest of us *real* Americans?"

Will flexed his jaw. "Settle down, Andie. I'm on your side here. I told you I'd look into it and I will. That's the best I can do right now."

"Right. Well, thanks for your time, Sheriff."

She slid out of the Bronco and walked back to her battered old truck with her head high. He frowned, watching her start up the truck and rumble down the road toward the Limber Pine.

Nothing but a whole lot of trouble in one hell of a package.

"What's he doing here?"

Carly Samuelson, the area game warden and Andie's close friend, glanced up from the jugs she and Andie were filling at the water fountain. Her long blond braid swung out as she followed Andie's gaze. "What's who doing here?"

"Will. The new sheriff." Andie hadn't seen him in more than a week, not since she'd stormed out of his Bronco after their visit to Jessop's ranch. The last possible place she'd expected to encounter him was at Whiskey Creek's annual end-of-summer softball tournament.

Somehow she'd forgotten in that time his impact on her, how just looking at him made her feel as if a thousand volts of electricity had pumped into her body.

It was bad enough when he was wearing his uniform. But she felt positively weak-kneed at the sight of him in jeans and a T-shirt throwing a softball to Emily and looking younger and more relaxed than she'd ever seen him.

"Will?" Carly asked. "You mean Beth's gorgeous big brother?"

"Shame on you, Carly." Andie laughed, though she wholeheartedly agreed. She briefly contemplated shoving her head under the icy stream of water in the fountain.

"Besides," she added, "you're a happily married woman with your own gorgeous man."

"He is, isn't he?" Carly practically purred as she watched her husband giving last-minute pointers to his team.

Chase must have felt them looking at him because he turned and grinned at both of them. Even from this distance Andie could see his dimples—the ones she and Carly teased him about—flashing. A former major league baseball player, Chase exuded masculine grace and strength. He was also one of the most caring men Andie had ever met, with a heart as big as the Wind Rivers. After his premature retirement, he'd returned to Whiskey Creek to convert his family's ranch into a camp that provided outdoors experience for children with juvenile-onset diabetes. Another one of his projects was this softball tournament. He organized it every year—this year with Carly's help—and hosted the barbecue that followed at their ranch.

Andie had been friends with him longer than his wife, since Carly had only returned to Whiskey Creek herself the previous summer. She'd grown up in the town, but her work as a fish and game officer had taken her all across the state. She had come back to the Wind Rivers area to investigate a rash of bear poachings. She'd ended up not only catching the poachers but marrying her old friend Chase.

Chase's gaze warmed now as he looked at his wife, and Andie felt awkward, excluded from their private communication. They acted as if they'd been married for just weeks instead of a year.

She busied herself with filling the other water jug. "So what about Will?" she asked Carly. "I didn't expect to see him here."

Carly jerked her attention from her husband. "Beth brought Emily out to the Lazy Jake one day last week, and she and a few of the campers hit it off. They talked her into coming to play in the games today, and she must have dragged her father along to watch." Her gaze became speculative. "Why the sudden interest in the whereabouts of our new sheriff?"

Andie flushed. "No reason. Just curious."

"Mmmm-hmmm." Carly grinned. "You know what they say about curiosity, honey."

"Meow," Andie murmured.

"So how's the new tenant working out, anyway."

"He mostly keeps to himself," she told Carly as they carried the jugs to the dugout Chase's team was using. "Sometimes I see him and Emily leave in the morning and pull in after dark, but that's about it."

She suspected he was purposely avoiding her. That was fine by her, she told herself. Especially after his callous attitude about the work camp.

The thought of the camp reminded her of Juana and Frederico, who had moved on the day after she and Will had visited. They'd stopped by the school before they left to tell her Jessop had mysteriously left what he owed them in an envelope on their doorstep—enough to pay the bill at the clinic with money left over to make their way to the orchards of Washington State.

Because of the timing of it, and because it seemed so out of character for Jessop, she wondered if Will could possibly have left the money. She'd probably never know, however. Even if he had been kind enough to make the gesture, she suspected he was the sort who would never admit it.

She couldn't help wondering, though, as she watched him stretch his lean length on the opposite side of the bleachers. He sent her a polite nod as the game started.

After a few quick looks beneath the cover of her eyelashes, Andie tried not to pay too much attention to him. She concentrated on the game instead, on the rich, sweet scent of freshly mowed grass, on the excited hum of the crowd, on the bad jokes of the announcer, dear old Jake Samuelson, Chase's grandfather.

Whiskey Creek's annual Labor Day Free-for-All had become one of her favorite events of the year. Everybody played in the tournament, from grandmothers to peewee leaguers. Whoever signed up in the morning had a chance to be on a team.

It was just one of the many traditions she loved about Whiskey Creek, a part of the brilliant, ever-changing flow of life in a small town. The Founders' Day parade, the volunteer fire department's annual pancake supper, the livestock auction the first Tuesday of every month that was more social than business. The harvest dances and the Halloween festivals and the modern-day barn raisings. She loved them all.

They celebrated life here, she thought. The changing of the seasons, births and deaths and comings of age.

Like any other place, Whiskey Creek had its problems, not the least of which was typical small-town closed mindedness about anything residents might consider different. But there was also a deep and abiding sense of community, of belonging, of being a vital portion of the greater whole.

She cheered hard for Emily in the fifth inning when the girl came up to bat and swatted a low fly ball that landed between the shortstop and the left fielder. Out of the corner of her eye, she saw Will on his feet, shouting encouragement to his daughter. When she headed to third base, bringing in a runner, Emily beamed as if she'd just led her team to the World Series title.

"I'm going to grab a hot dog," Andie told Carly once the excitement died down. "Can I get you anything?"

Carly shook her head. "No, thanks."

"Save my spot!"

Keeping one eye on the action, she made her way to the concession stand. It took her twice as long as it should have to walk to the soft-drink trailer in the parking lot mainly because so many people stopped her along the route to say hello.

And when she was only ten yards away, a beefy hand landed on her shoulder. She turned to find Tom Jessop glowering at her.

"Tom," she greeted him coolly.

He dropped his hand and glared at her. "I hear you been stickin' your nose where it don't belong again."

"If that's what you want to call it, yes, I have."

"Stay the hell off my land, you hear me?"

"Half the county hears you, Tom," she murmured, trying to keep a cool head. What frustrated her more than anything else about the situation was that Tom was one of the wealthiest ranchers in the community. He could certainly afford to upgrade his workers' housing. He just chose not to.

"I mean it," he said. "You cost me two of my best workers, damn you. The rest of 'em are telling me they're movin' on too. What the hell am I supposed to do now? It's all your fault for buttin' in where you got no business."

At the thought of Juana Flores and her husband and children living in that dilapidated shack, Andie gave up the battle to keep her temper under control.

"If you wouldn't treat your workers like slaves, maybe you could keep them for longer than a few days. Don't blame me, Tom, just because you're a lousy excuse for an employer and an even poorer excuse for a human being."

His florid face reddened even more. "Why you . . ." He loomed menacingly over her, but Andie held her ground, even though her heart was pounding like a stampede.

"Back off, Jessop." Will's voice, calm and unruffled, broke into the tense silence.

The rancher turned to him. "You stay out of this, Tanner. You're a newcomer here and I got no beef with you, even though you did trespass on my land. This is between me and the little lady here."

"Okay. You've said your piece now and so has the 'little lady.'" He flashed an almost grin at Andie. "Now go on back to your ranch and settle down."

Tom's thick hands clenched. "You keep her away from my help, Sheriff," he said. "If I catch her messin' in my business again, it'll be the last time. Understand?"

Instantly, Will was in the other man's face, his own expression fierce. "Understand this, Jessop. She gets hurt, so much as a broken fingernail, I'll know right where to come looking. Understand?"

"Dad. What's going on?"

Andie turned at the voice of Jessop's teenage son, Marty. He gave her a shy, surreptitious smile, and she managed to smile back. Though he took after his father in size and appearance, Marty had a quiet, amiable nature. That's why she couldn't understand how he made her so uncomfortable.

Since the Rocking J was just down the road from the Limber Pine, he sometimes stopped when he was passing by to ask if she needed help with anything, and she always wanted to escape into the house whenever she saw him. Maybe it was the way he sometimes looked at her with a little more interest than an eighteen-year-old ought to have for someone nearly twice his age. Still, she put that down to teenage hormones.

"Nothing's going on, son," Jessop said. "I'm just having a nice little chat about trespassing with Miz McPhee and the new sheriff here."

His son's presence seemed to defuse Jessop's anger, and after another glare at Andie and Will, he let Marty lead him away.

"I saw him head over here," Will said to Andie when they were alone, "and was afraid he had trouble on his mind."

So Will *had* been watching her. She thought she'd felt his gaze as she headed toward the concession stand, but hadn't wanted to turn around to be sure.

"You didn't need to rescue me, Sheriff," she said. "I was doing just fine."

"I know you were. I just didn't want to have to pick up the pieces when you were done with him."

She chuckled, then reaction abruptly set in. "I—I need to sit down. My knees are still shaking. I thought he was going to slug me for a minute there."

She made it to a patch of grass, and he squatted down beside her. "So did I. Listen, Andie, stay away from the Rocking J. Let me handle the rest of the investigation. Jessop doesn't strike me as the kind of guy who's going to give up easily. If you see or hear anything suspicious, let me know."

She closed her eyes and heard again the garbled voice of her tormenting caller. She really ought to tell Will about it, she thought. Then again, she hadn't had any calls for several days. Maybe the whole thing was over.

"Feeling any better?" he asked after a few more minutes.

"I think so."

He reached a hand to help her up, and without thinking Andie clasped it. As he pulled her to her feet, their gazes locked. Breathless, she watched his eyes darken, felt the heat of his skin, the strength of his fingers. The yells and shouts of the crowd seemed to shimmer away, leaving only the two of them.

"Andie—" he started to say, but before he could complete the sentence, an anxious yell sounded behind them.

"Sheriff Tanner!"

They both turned, and Andie watched Joey Whitehorse climb out of his sheriff's department Bronco and run toward them.

She glanced at Will and was shocked at the change in him. He was instantly on alert, his features tense, looking for all the world like a wolf scenting trouble.

"What's wrong, Joe?"

"Miz Walker just called the office trying to find you." The deputy was breathless when he reached them. "She says Jace went after range cows this morning, and she can't round him up on the cellular and she's afraid the baby's coming."

Will was racing for his Jeep before Joe finished speaking. Andie rushed after him. "I'm coming with you," she said.

"You don't need to."

"She's my friend. I want to help, if I can."

Shouts from the ball diamond suddenly distracted him, and they both turned just in time to see Emily catch a fly ball.

"Damn," Will muttered. "I forgot about Emily. What am I going to do with her?"

"Will, this is Whiskey Creek. Give me two minutes and I'll find somebody completely trustworthy to take her for the night."

She raced back to Carly on the bleachers.

"I was wondering what happened to you," her friend said. "There must be a huge line."

"I don't have time to explain everything right now, but Beth thinks she's in labor, and Will and I are going out to the Bar W to help. Can Emily spend the night at the Lazy Jake?"

"Of course!" Carly said instantly. "Is there anything else we can do?"

"Just pray Beth waits until she makes it to the hospital to have this baby."

SIX

Later, Andie had almost no recollection of the frenzied drive to the Bar W, just vague impressions of a white-knuckled Will and the pines rushing by in a blur as they sped to the ranch.

They squealed into the driveway, and she jumped out of the Jeep before it even rolled to a complete stop. Without bothering to knock, she rushed inside, Will close behind her.

"Beth? Honey, where are you?"

"I'm in here," Beth called out, though her voice that normally bubbled over with enthusiasm was thin and strained. Andie followed the sound to the living room and found Beth perched on the couch, pale but composed.

"Is your bag packed?" Will asked.

"It's over there," she said calmly. "I don't know if it will do us any good, though. I don't think there's time to make it to Jackson."

"First babies generally take a while to get here," Andie said.

"I know. That's what I told myself when the contractions started this morning. And then my water broke fifteen minutes ago."

What little color she had left in her face disappeared suddenly, and Beth doubled over on the couch, holding her distended abdomen and panting as if she'd just run a marathon in record time.

Andie rushed to her and put a supportive arm around her. "Ride it out, honey. Just breathe." She tried to remember the breathing exercises she'd learned so long ago, the ones she'd never been able to use.

"How far apart are they?" Will asked, when the contraction ended.

"Not nearly far enough," Beth muttered and Andie squeezed her hand. "About two minutes."

He frowned. "How regular?"

"Well, I haven't missed one for the last two hours. They seem to be getting stronger since my water broke."

Will muttered an oath, worry furrowing his forehead, his silver-gray eyes murky and troubled. "You're probably close. Why in the hell did you wait this long to call somebody?"

"Don't yell at me, big brother," she snapped. "I've never had a baby before. I thought they were just Braxton Hicks contractions, like I've been having for a month. I'm three weeks early, after all. How was I supposed to know this is the real enchilada?"

"It's not your fault." Andie aimed a glare at Will. "You didn't know. The question is, what are we going to do about it?"

"As I see it, we have two choices," Will said. "We

can head into Jackson ourselves. That's an hour's drive and we'd be running the risk that the kid might decide to make an appearance while we're on the road. Or we can call for an ambulance to take her, then at least she'd have somebody with a hell of a lot more medical training than I have."

"Whiskey Creek doesn't have an ambulance," Andie said. "We've raised all the money for it, but it won't arrive for another month."

"I don't think I can wait that long," Beth said helpfully.

"Damn," Will said. "Where's the closest one?"

"Over in Pinedale. Still a half hour away."

Beth suddenly stiffened and groaned.

"Another one?" Andie asked. Her friend nodded and resumed her breathing exercises.

"They're coming closer," Will said. "Beth, let's get you in the other room where you can lie down." As soon as the contraction was over, he lifted his sister off the couch. Andie saw his mouth twitch with the added burden on his bad shoulder.

"William Charles Tanner," Beth exclaimed, "put me down. I'm having a baby. I didn't break my leg. I'm perfectly capable of walking."

"Be quiet and breathe, brat," he said, and headed into the bedroom. Andie followed and watched him lay his sister on the bed.

"Andie, call the Whiskey Creek doctor—what's his name, Matthews—and tell him I want him here yesterday. Tell him to call Pinedale for an ambulance and have them meet us here. While you're at it, try Jace's cellular phone again. And then I'll need some towels and some string and some hot water."

"Just like on TV?"

He flashed her a grin that, under other circumstances, would have stolen her breath. "That's right, sweetheart. Just like on TV. Now let's see if I've watched this enough times—and remember enough of my police training—to know what I'm doing."

Andie hurried into the kitchen to use the phone, her breathing ragged. What if something went wrong with the baby? There were so many possible complications. She didn't dare give voice to her panic, though. Beth was going to have a tough enough time without Andie worrying her further.

Her fingers fumbling, she punched in the number for the Whiskey Creek clinic and sagged with relief when old Dr. Matthews himself answered.

"Somehow I knew that girl was going to pull something like this," he said after promising Andie he was on his way.

She had no luck trying to reach Jace, though. He must be too high in the mountains for his phone to work, she thought. When that man finally turned up, she planned to chew him out thoroughly for leaving his pregnant wife for the day.

Andie finally gave up and hung up the phone. As she stood there, her hand on the cool plastic receiver, she was consumed with a frantic, primeval longing for her mother. Leticia, in her brisk, competent manner, would know all about the right kinds of herbs to have on hand in this kind of emergency, both antiseptic and anesthetic. Maybe she could just call her . . .

You're stalling, Andie, she thought as she leaned against the wall and closed her eyes. The wild panic that had been nipping at her since she ran into the ranch house began to growl in earnest. She couldn't do this. She *couldn't*. She wanted to escape to the safety of her own house, away from Beth's pain, away from the breathing and the pushing.

Away from the baby.

The baby. Andie felt her breathing accelerate, her lungs begin to suck in tortured gasps of air, and she dug her fingernails into her palms. Slowly, steadily, she forced herself to calm down.

She was stronger than this, dammit. She had to be, for Beth's sake and for her own. Summoning all her energy, she walked to the sink, poured a glass of water, and drained it in one quick motion. Her hands shaking, she splashed frigid water on her face, then washed her hands and gathered the supplies Will needed.

Drawing one more unsteady breath, she left the kitchen. She could do this. She *would* do this.

In the end, Andie did little more than watch. Will astounded her with his gentleness, his easy competence. He squeezed Beth's hand when she needed it and wiped the sweat from her forehead. He was calm and cool, everything Andie wasn't.

"I need to push," Beth moaned.

"Don't push, sweetheart," he said. "Not yet. Just breathe for a little while longer. The doctor will be here any second now. That's it, sweetheart. You're doing just great."

The bawling of cows outside distracted Andie from the drama unfolding before her, and she glanced out the window to see Jace riding hell for leather down the hillside. Several hundred yards behind him a couple of the Bar W hands were driving in the herd of about sixty range cows, but the distance between Jace and the herd lengthened with each powerful stride of his mount.

"Is that my husband?" Beth asked. Her face was pale, her red hair plastered to her forehead.

"Yeah." Andie was already heading for the door.

"I want him in here now so I can kill him."

"You'll have to wait in line, honey. I'm first."

"I'll take a shot at what's left of him," Will said, "but after we get this baby here."

Jace slid off his lathered horse just as Andie opened the front door. "I saw the Jeep when we topped the hill," he panted. "It was parked all wrong, with the door wide open, like somebody rushed out in one hell of a hurry. What's the matter? Is it Beth?"

"Your child's about to be born. Where in the blue blazes have you been?"

He opened his mouth to reply, panic flitting across his handsome features, but she grabbed him by the front of his denim work shirt and hauled him inside.

"It doesn't matter," she said. "You're here now. But I'm not going to let you touch her or that baby until you shower off this horse sweat and God knows what else is all over you. Move it, buster."

Jace made it, just barely.

"The baby's crowning," Will said, just as his brother-in-law rushed into the bedroom in clean clothes. "Beth, honey, it looks like we're on our own with this one."

"I have to push, Will. I'm sorry," she whimpered.

"Okay, sweetheart. Give it all you've got. Great. Great! Just one more and we're there. Thatta girl. There you go. . . . There you go . . ." With a mighty heave, the baby slid out in a slick mess onto the towels Will had padded up underneath Beth.

"Oh my Lord," Jace breathed, his face paling.

The baby squawked at the indignity of it all. "You have a son," Will exclaimed. "Ten fingers, ten toes. One head."

He laughed exultantly, even as he wiped his face on his shoulder. Andie didn't know if he was wiping tears or sweat. It didn't seem to matter. She felt numb, her emotions frozen, even as she felt the tears coursing down her own cheeks.

"Oh my Lord," Jace repeated. He gathered his wife into his arms, and the two of them stared at the tiny thing they had created.

Andie didn't realize she was edging away from the tableau on the bed until her shoulders bumped against the far wall. She stiffened and took a step forward while Will quickly, efficiently cleaned up the child and wrapped him in a receiving blanket from Beth's hospital bag. He handed him to his parents just as a bustle sounded from the doorway.

"Looks like, as usual, I missed the fun part." Old Doc Matthews, his white hair windblown and his old-fashioned leather medical bag in hand, ambled into the room. "Trust you, Beth Walker, to do things your own way."

"Sorry, Doc," she said weakly, still in the circle of Jace's arms.

"Looks like that fancy specialist I sent you to in Jackson was one big waste of time and money. The sheriff here did just fine without either one of us."

"The sheriff never wants to go through something

like this again," Will said, just as the scream of an ambulance set the baby crying again.

Just hang on. It's almost over, Andie told herself as she slipped from the room to usher in the paramedics with their stretcher. It only took a few minutes for them to pack Beth and the baby on the stretcher and wheel her through the ranch house.

She should have known, though, that she wouldn't be able to escape that easily. Beth caught sight of her as they were nearly to the door. "Wait," she commanded the paramedics. They obediently stopped.

"Did you see him, Andie?" she asked.

Andie gathered the last fragments of her control and walked through the crowd of men to the stretcher. She could hardly see the child, he was so wrapped up in the blanket. She caught only a glimpse of red skin, puckered-up eyes, and a tiny cupid's bow of a mouth. It was enough. And too much.

"You did good, kid," she said through the ache in her throat, brushing Beth's hair from her forehead.

"He's beautiful, isn't he?" Tears welled in her friend's eyes as she cradled her child, and Andie smiled softly, though her heart felt as if it had cracked apart and shattered into a million pieces.

"The most beautiful baby I've ever seen."

In a flurry of activity, the paramedics wheeled Beth out the door, and suddenly the house was as quiet as death. Alone, Andie closed her eyes and drew in a shaky breath. Work. She needed to work. Anything to take her mind from the images crowding through it.

She hurried into the bedroom and stripped off the soiled linens and, with more force than the job called for, shook out a clean sheet with a powerful snap. She was throwing on the top sheet when Will appeared, his broad shoulders filling the doorway.

"Hi," he said quietly.

"Hi yourself," she answered. She leaned to tuck in a bottom corner, avoiding his gaze. "You did good, too, back there."

"Beth did all the work."

"She's lucky to have had you."

He rubbed at his bad shoulder, unconsciously, she was sure. "Well, Jace wants to ride in the ambulance, so I'm going to follow them in their truck so he has transportation in Jackson. Doc Matthews will give me a ride back home."

"Okay."

He paused. "If you can drive my Jeep back to the ranch, I can take you to town to pick up your truck tonight or tomorrow morning."

"Okay," she said again.

He was watching her carefully. Too carefully. She turned away to tuck in the other corner.

"Are you sure you're all right?"

"Sure," she lied, praying she could make it home before she broke down completely. "Why on earth wouldn't I be?"

No welcoming lights greeted Will when Doc Matthews dropped him at the Limber Pine Ranch close to midnight. Buzzing with exhaustion, he felt a moment's panic surge through him. Where was Andie? Usually she left on a porch light, but now only pearly rays from the full moon shimmered in the night.

She probably just fell asleep after the stress of the day, he told himself.

The dogs ran out to greet him, and he took a moment to give attention to each one, as they'd come to expect. It seemed like a lifetime since he'd been able to enjoy the simple, pure pleasures of soft dog fur between his fingers, the calming sight of moonlight bathing the tops of the pine trees. The wondrous miracle of new life.

He drew in a sharp breath as the reminder of his new nephew brought an ache to his chest. Through the ordeal of the delivery and the long drive to the hospital and back, he'd purposely shunted aside all the pain seeing that child summoned in him.

Now, though, with his defenses down, he could feel all the memories of Sarah and their baby gathering force to attack.

In an effort to divert himself, he started on his nightly walk around the ranch. It had become a ritual with him, a calming, relaxing practice to walk the length of Andie's well-kept property each evening.

Heading along the west fence, he crossed the footbridge over the irrigation ditch and walked down around the far pasture. A barn owl called somewhere overhead, and the wind mourned through the treetops, but otherwise all was quiet.

He closed his eyes, inhaling the intoxicating scent of flowers—of fresh growth—that permeated the entire ranch. For some reason, all his emotions felt close to the surface tonight. He felt as if he'd spent the last three years in a numb daze, immersed in Novocain, that was just now beginning to wear off.

He was heading back toward the house and the

cottage when he saw her. Just a shadow in moonlight, she was curled up on the garden bench, her arms wrapped tightly around herself.

He stared. "Andie? What are you doing out here? It's past midnight."

She didn't answer his call, and unease stirred to life inside him. "Andie?"

"Go away," she said, her voice so low he barely heard.

He ignored the order and walked closer, then stopped abruptly. What he saw shook him clear through. His calm, unflappable Andie—who could take on a roomful of wild preschoolers or an angry rancher without blinking an eye—looked as if she was a heartbeat away from total hysteria.

"What's wrong? Has something happened?"

"Nothing's wrong. Go away, Will. Just go away. Please?"

He squatted down so he could see her eyes. The anguish there, raw like a gaping wound, stunned him. She made a soft, mewling sound, and before he could think it through, he pulled her off the bench and into his arms, unable to bear her misery.

"Shhh, baby. Don't cry." She only cried harder, the sobs shuddering through her body in jerky waves. "What's the matter? I can't help you, Andie, unless you tell me."

"They're gone. All of them. Gone."

"Who's gone?"

It was a long time before she answered, and when she did her voice was as fragile as a rose petal. "I thought I could be strong, Will, but I can't."

"You are. You're one of the strongest women I've

ever met. Look at all you do—running the Limber Pine by yourself and the school. And taking care of everybody in Whiskey Creek, whether they want you to or not."

"It's a lie. All of it."

"What happened, Andie?" he asked softly. "Can you talk about it?"

Her cheek nestled against his chest and he patted her hair awkwardly, wishing he knew what to do to ease her pain.

"I've tried so hard to be happy for Beth," she said, "and I am. I truly am, Will. She's wanted this baby forever and she's my best friend and I wanted her to have her dream. I could handle it, I told myself. I've had a long time to deal with it. But I can't. It hurts. Oh, Will, it hurts."

He didn't know what to say, so he just brushed his hand through her hair again and held her while she sobbed, questions swirling around inside him.

After a few minutes, her shoulders heaved as she struggled for control, then she took a deep breath and pulled away from him. "I'm sorry. You're very good with hysterical women, you know."

He gave a ragged laugh. "I do my best. You want to tell me what this is all about?"

"No, I don't. If I tell you, you'll know what a terrible, selfish person I am."

"I could never think that. Tell me, Andie."

She sighed and sat down again, pulling her knees to her chest, her arms wrapped around them protectively. She stared out at her darkened garden for a long time before answering, and when she spoke, it was barely above a whisper.

"I—I was married before. You know that, right?"

He nodded, remembering her talking about meeting her husband at college and wondering briefly why that bothered him so much.

"I . . . We tried. To have children, I mean. Peter wanted a son desperately. It was like an obsession with him. He—he came from a very important family. Old money. They wanted a new Stansfield to carry on the family name." Her voice quivered with bitterness.

"I got pregnant right away, and for the first time since Peter and I got engaged I felt as if his family accepted me. His parents had had some blue-blood debutante picked out for him. I'm afraid a half-Guatemalan, half-Irish schoolteacher just didn't fit their plans." She gave a travesty of a smile and continued. "I didn't much care, but it was hard on Peter, their disapproval. So I was happy for him when they began to mellow after they learned I was pregnant."

She looked out into the night, at something he couldn't see. "It was a boy, we found out. We planned to name him Christopher." She paused. "When I was eight months along, I started bleeding. They did a Caesarean but he . . . he was already dead. I'd wondered why I hadn't felt him move for several days."

It was eerie how calmly she spoke the words, Will thought. As if she were reciting a grocery list or a TV schedule.

He reached for her again, but she shrugged him off and hugged her arms tighter around her legs. "The doctors said it was just one of those things. They didn't know why it happened. We'll try again, I thought. I was young. We had plenty of time. But I—I miscarried another baby six months later, when I was three months along. A girl that time. And then eight months after that, another boy."

He couldn't bear it, couldn't stand the anguish threading through her voice. "Andie, stop. You don't have to tell me anymore."

"I thought I was over it, Will. It was years ago, after all, and I thought I could be strong. So today I—I decided I wanted to give Beth some of the things I'd saved. I went to the attic and opened the box of baby clothes, and I found this." She held up a knitted baby blanket, blue with yellow teddy bears on it, and Will's chest ached when he saw the tears sliding down her face.

"I knitted it for Christopher, spent months on it. I'm a lousy knitter, you know." She gave a watery laugh. "But I wanted to make something special for him. For my son."

Why was she telling him this? Andie wondered. Once the words started, she couldn't seem to stop them. They gushed out like the first churning surge of water spilling from the irrigation canal when she opened the diversion gate every summer.

She couldn't tell him the rest, how the last failed pregnancy had been all her body could take. The terrible time in the hospital after the tubal pregnancy burst her fallopian tube, the infection that had raged for weeks, forcing the doctors to take her womb in order to save her life.

The children she would never have.

Andie stared out at her garden. It sounded so melodramatic put like that. She would never bear a child, but that didn't mean she was any less of a person, any less of a woman. Despite the fact that Peter's parents had somehow convinced him otherwise.

"People never knew what to say to me," she went on. "That was the worst. They always said they understood what I was going through. But how could they? No one knows, unless they've lost a child, how it gouges out your heart to look at a mother pushing a child in a stroller. How your arms always, *always*, feel empty."

Something about his silence drew her attention, and Andie was shocked to see his face set in a stony mask.

Suddenly she remembered his son, the child who had died unborn along with Will's wife. Shame at her own self-pity washed through her. All day she had been so consumed with her own pain, she hadn't given one single thought to what he must be going through.

He had lost so much. Yet he had managed to work past his own heartache to help his sister. How he must have struggled to be so calm and efficient back at the ranch while he delivered the child.

"Oh, Will," she said. "I'm sorry. So sorry." Acting entirely on instinct, spurred only by a need to comfort him, to wipe that grief from his eyes, she stood and wrapped her arms around him. For a moment he held his arms out to his sides, as if afraid to touch her, then he clutched her fiercely, like a drowning man grabbing a lifeline.

SEVEN

For a long time she held him there in her garden, his face buried in the crook of her neck while the night wind whispered in the trees, and the air, lush with the scent of a thousand blossoms, eddied around them.

Grief seemed to seep from him, rippling, shuddering out. Her own anguish carefully locked away once again, Andie clutched his back, his hair, longing to heal him, to absorb his pain inside her.

She thought of his word that morning in her garden when she'd asked what he was looking for. *Atonement.* As if it had been his fault his wife and his son had died.

He didn't deserve to lose so much. A wife. A son. His innocence and idealism, all in one fell swoop. He'd only been doing his job, fighting for peace in a violent world. She hurt to think of it, to think of him blaming himself for what had been a cruel act of vengeance.

Slowly his shuddering eased and he relaxed in her arms, then pulled away.

"You're very good with hysterical men," he said, repeating her words.

She laughed softly. "Thank you."

Then, as she'd somehow known he would, he dipped his head and kissed her. Gently. Sweetly. A kiss meant only for thanks, for comfort, but she couldn't stop the sigh of pleasure that whispered from her parted lips. It felt wonderful. Wonderful and *right*, like the first snowflakes in the winter, the first budding plants in the spring.

The tight, clawing bands of pain around her heart loosened and broke away; her muscles and sinews relaxed as if she'd shed a heavy coat of armor.

How long had it been since she'd known the healing comfort of simply being held by another person? Of a heartbeat pulsing the cadence of life against her chest? Of skin and hair beneath her fingers, rich and warm and brimming with life? Of his breath mingling with hers until she didn't know where he ended and she began?

She wanted to stay right there forever, in the comfort of his arms, with his lips merged with hers.

He deepened the kiss, his mouth firm on hers, and she tightened her arms around him, loving the rough, hard textures of him, the solid, unyielding strength. Her movement brought her closer to him, and Andie could feel his heat through the thin material of her nightgown.

Suddenly the kiss took on another, more primitive meaning. She held her breath as her nipples swelled and seemed to catch on the cotton gown, her breasts aching with a deep, ancient need.

An instant before she would have rubbed against

him, she realized what was happening. She froze, horrified at herself, at her own helpless response, at the pulsing arousal that seemed to surge out of nowhere like a flash flood violently pounding through a desert arroyo.

She inched back from him, pulling her mouth away, disentangling her arms from around his neck.

What on earth was she thinking? She closed her eyes and took a shallow, shuddering breath, struggling for control. And where had all these glittering, alive sensations come from?

When she opened her eyes, she found his face inches away, his gaze fierce and unwavering. Time seemed to pause, shimmering between them, then he reached for her, engulfing her in the tight haven of his arms.

There was little of gentleness this time. His mouth was hot and turbulent on hers. Urgent, demanding. Arousing.

She should be protesting this, she thought. Should be putting up some token resistance, about how she wasn't the sort of woman who rolled in the grass with a man who'd never acted as if he wanted anything more from her than an odd, stilted friendship. But he weaved such magic with his mouth and his hands, promised such healing, such nurturing, she could do nothing but meet him kiss for kiss, taste for taste.

He lowered her onto the cool grass, his mouth fused with hers, his hands buried in her hair. She felt the length of him against her, felt his hardness, such a heady, intoxicating contrast to her own curves.

He kissed her for what felt like forever—and yet

not nearly long enough—until she was panting with need.

When he finally lifted a hand and slid it to one aching breast, when he cupped her in his big, hard hand and flitted his thumb across her nipple, Andie thought she would burn away into cinders.

She arched against him, and slowly, agonizingly slowly, he worked free the fastenings of her gown. The quiet rasp of each button sliding through the buttonhole, the feel of his rough fingers brushing her skin, sent erotic tremors through her. Finally he undid the last one.

He eased himself away from her, his face expressionless as he studied her in the moonlight. For a moment—an awful, heart-stopping instant—Andie was terrified he would jerk away again, as he had that night in his kitchen.

I don't want you.

She braced herself for it and held her breath. *I don't want you.*

"You're beautiful," he said, his voice husky, aroused. "So damn beautiful, Andie. I can't even think straight when I'm around you."

Weak with relief as his low words strummed through her, she exhaled on a shaky sigh.

He had been lying that night. With a calm assurance, she knew it, that he had been fighting this wild heat between them as fiercely as she had been. It seemed so pointless now, like two people trying to hold back the stars or hide the sun. Their coming together was inevitable. It had been since that night in his kitchen.

She smiled gently as he watched her through those

uncanny wolf eyes. "You're not so bad yourself, Sheriff," she whispered.

He groaned and pulled her up to him, but she wedged her hands between them to unbutton his shirt. With trembling fingers, she drew it off his shoulders and nearly moaned at the glowing heat of his bare skin. She could feel his heart race, and she closed her eyes as she lay her hand flat against his hard chest, feeling his life's blood pulsing, strong and swift, beneath the light matting of hair.

She spread her fingers out to explore him and felt him stiffen just as her little finger encountered something that didn't quite feel right. Lowering her head for a closer look, she could barely make out through the dark the angry evidence of his recent wound, a nickel-sized scar just beneath the ridge of his collarbone. Her gaze flew to his, then down again to the scar.

"Oh, Will," she whispered. "I'm so sorry." Then gently, gently, she pressed her lips there, wishing she could kiss away the pain she knew still bothered him.

He moaned, and she felt it rumble beneath her mouth, then he pulled her up, burying his fingers in her hair, and meshed his mouth with hers. The movement pressed her bare skin to his, and this time she rubbed against him as his tongue licked and teased at her lips until she opened for him.

In one smooth motion, he slid off her nightgown, leaving her only in panties. Mindful of her own scars that crisscrossed her abdomen, she was enormously grateful for the concealing darkness.

He lowered her to the grass again and she felt its

soft embrace beneath her as his hardness pressed her into the ground.

"No fair, Sheriff," she whispered against his mouth when he reached down to remove her last flimsy layer of clothing. "You're still half-dressed."

"It's only a matter of time, sweetheart. Trust me," he whispered back, and she gave a shaky laugh that ended in a low, gasping moan as he lowered his head to take one swollen nipple between his lips.

She arched beneath him, her hands clasping him to her, as he suckled, taking his time with each one. With each touch, a burning need spiraled inside her. She clasped his back, skimming her hands over his skin until she found a scar to match the one on the front that felt angry and puckered. She would have kissed that one, too, but she couldn't reach it, so she contented herself with gliding her mouth against his shoulder, tasting the saltiness of his skin, inhaling the cedar-and-pine scent of him.

Slowly, agonizingly slowly, he slid his hand inside the waistband of her panties, his mouth still fastened on one breast, and danced his fingers across the sensitive nub of flesh hidden in her curls. Sparkling heat spread through her at the feel of his big rough hand on the most intimate part of her. Teasing her. Stroking her. Inflaming her.

She felt as if she were caught up in a wild wind, twirling amid the treetops like a feather on a current of air. Faster, faster the wind tossed her. Higher, higher. Just as he dipped a finger inside her, as she touched the sun in a blinding flash of light, she screamed his name.

Slowly, she fluttered back to the ground to find

he'd removed his jeans and was kneeling between her legs, his face dark with need.

He paused, his body taut, his muscles flexed, and she couldn't quite figure out why, until her gaze met his. He was waiting for her to grant him permission to give them both the complete intimacy their bodies craved.

After what he had just given her—after the magical, wondrous world he'd just shown her—did he really think she would want to deny him anything? She smiled and drew his mouth to hers, answering his wordless plea with one of her own.

"Are you sure?" Will asked gruffly, his blood thick and heavy in his veins. He would have died if she'd said no. As it was, he felt as if he were teetering on the precipice of control.

Through the dark he thought he saw her nod her head. It was all the answer he needed and he groaned, then plunged into her with one powerful motion.

At the feel of her sheathing him, her hot, silken depths surrounding him, welcoming him, all his careful restraint sizzled away, leaving only the pulsing urgency that thrummed through him.

He wanted to move slowly, to make it satisfying for her. He tried. Damn if he didn't try. But all he could focus on was the way she felt so good against him, around him, tight and slick and welcoming. The way her body arched under him. The way her mouth parted a little more with each thrust of his body inside her.

Beyond conscious thought, he grasped her hands in his and lowered his mouth to catch her erotic gasps of arousal. She kissed him back, pressing her mouth against his again and again, and he thrust his tongue inside, a simulation of the motion of his body. She raked her teeth against him, and he completely lost any hold on his sanity.

With one last, tremendous surge, he felt the world explode, felt her muscles contract around him as he found release.

When he could think again, he realized his face was buried in her hair, the dark curls surrounding him with the lavender-and-vanilla scent that clung to her. For a moment he had an odd feeling, one he struggled to recognize. Finally it came to him. Peace. He closed his eyes and savored the sensation. For the first time in three years, he felt at peace, cleansed by the fire of her arms.

But at what cost? He lifted his head and saw in the moonlight her eyes were tightly closed, her lashes fanning her cheeks. Guilt rushed through him and he rolled off her, staring up at the stars that dotted the sky like tiny pinpricks in black paper.

What kind of animal was he to attack her when she was in such emotional agony? And outside in the grass, for hell's sake.

Just when he thought he couldn't stoop any lower in life, he'd managed to dig an even deeper hole for himself. How could he possibly face her now, knowing he'd taken advantage of her pain, of her soft vulnerability, to appease his aching hunger for her.

He sat up and scrubbed his hands over his face, not daring to look at her. He was very much afraid if he saw her now, limned in moonlight like a beautiful alabaster goddess, nothing would stop him from taking her again.

"I'm sorry, Andie," he muttered. "I lost control. It's been . . . a long time for me."

"Don't you dare apologize to me, Will Tanner." He winced at the fury in her voice. She had every right to despise him.

But why did it bother him so much that the woman he'd been trying to avoid for a month now likely wouldn't want to have a thing to do with him? It's what he wanted, wasn't it?

"That's the only thing I can say. I'm sorry. It won't happen again."

Even as he spoke the words, Will felt a wrenching sense of loss. In her arms, inside her body, he'd felt alive, his senses and his emotions humming with energy for the first time in three years. And now she hated him.

"I should never have taken advantage of you, of your pain," he said gruffly, trying to find his jeans in the shadows while self-contempt broiled inside him.

To his shock, her low laugh rippled through the night, and he jerked his gaze from the ground to her face.

"Who took advantage of whom here, Will Tanner?" Her smile was seductive and sweet at the same time. "I wanted you, wanted that. Good grief, I have since the day you moved in. You, with that stubborn streak as big as the Wind Rivers and your surly get-out-of-my-face attitude. Don't you dare apologize."

He stared. "Are you sure? I didn't give you much time to make up your mind back there."

"Will, I'm sure. I have absolutely no regrets. Except that we didn't make love sooner."

Relief flooded through him, then he was struck by

another thought. "I was so out of control I didn't even have enough sense to ask about protection."

She bit her lip and looked away. "You don't have to worry about that," she said softly.

She shivered suddenly, and he realized the air had reached the dew point. The grass beneath his feet was moist and cool, and a chill wind was sweeping down from Lone Eagle Peak.

He spied her nightgown, a pool of white against the darker grass, and he reached for it. She felt fragile in his arms again as he slid the nightgown over her body.

"You're cold. You'd better go on inside."

"Not unless you're coming with me," she said.

Doubts and misgivings and lingering regret battled inside him, but one look at her there in the moonlight swept them all away. He wanted that peace again. Just one more time. Was that too much to ask?

"A whole damn herd of Jace's mean old range cows couldn't keep me away," he vowed, and followed her into the house.

Frowning in frustration, Andie reached again underneath a vine for a particularly stubborn acorn squash. No matter how hard she pulled it, the blasted thing didn't want to budge. She had it in her hand, she could move it an inch or two either way, but she couldn't pluck it free of the tangled growth.

"Come on out, buster, or I'll leave you in there to rot," she muttered. Finally she tried sheer muscle and, grunting with effort, tugged on the thing. With one last tremendous heave she yanked it free and ended up on her backside in the dirt.

Score one for the garden, she thought, chuckling despite her awkward position.

Any other Sunday morning she would be relishing this quiet time, one of the only days she didn't have to hurry through her gardening to make it to the preschool. Today, though, try as she might, the solace she usually found here among her plants was as elusive as that darned squash. Her thoughts were completely consumed with the man currently sprawled in her bed.

Oh, mercy. She had a man sprawled in her bed.

Andie slid off her work gloves and rubbed a hand through her hair. Not just any man, either. Oh no, when she decided to break her five years of celibacy, she did it with a vengeance. With the blankets tucked around his hips and his brown hair mussed, Will had been so appealing she practically had to use a crowbar to get herself out of bed. But she needed this space, this distance, to come to terms with what had happened between them.

She glanced at the grass near her garden bench. She could find no trace of their wild passion there, but she didn't need any physical evidence. It was forever etched in her mind, from his first healing kiss of comfort to the fiery heat that had followed it. And the long hours of the night they'd spent entangled in each other's arms in the soft comfort of her bed.

Her cheeks burned as she remembered coming to life with Will. She'd been married three years, and she'd never once known making love could be so . . . shattering.

How could she not have known? How could she

have reached the age of thirty-two without any clue she could burn like that? Or that she had the ability with her touch to make someone else catch fire as Will had?

She heard again the echo of his voice, rough with passion, as he groaned out her name. Felt again the rasp of his stubbled cheeks against her neck, against her breasts. Tasted again the salty sweetness of his skin as she'd explored him.

"Good morning."

Andie jerked around, nearly tumbling the bushel basket brimming with vegetables. Will, his shoulder propped against the edge of the barn, stood watching her. The man moved like a blasted ghost. How long had he been there? She flushed. Had he seen her yelling at her vegetables and then her ignominious trip to the ground?

"Good morning," she replied, looking away.

"Why didn't you wake me?"

"I figured you needed your rest," she said, though that was only part of the truth. She wasn't quite sure how to deal with him this morning. Slipping out of bed and escaping to her garden had seemed the prudent course.

"I did need my rest," he said. "It's the first decent night's sleep I've had in a long time. Thank you."

He watched her out of those silver-gray eyes, and she busied herself with the vegetables.

"I called the hospital while you were sleeping," she said. "Both mama and baby are doing fine after a restful night. I told her maybe we could all come out later this afternoon. I hope that's okay with you."

"You don't have to do that. I know it's hard for

you. The baby and all. Don't put yourself through more than you can handle."

She smiled at his concern, warmed in ways she couldn't even begin to count.

"I'm okay, Will. Honest. Yesterday was a little overwhelming, but I feel much better now."

He looked unconvinced. "What about the rest of it? About us?"

She paused, then spoke truthfully. "I'm okay with that too. How about you?"

"I don't know. The memory's dimming."

The man grinned. He actually grinned! Andie stared at him, stunned by this side of him, this warm and playful man who must have been hiding inside the gruff and stoic soldier.

She cleared her throat and stepped forward, slipping her arms around him. "Maybe I could refresh it for you."

He grinned again, and the sunlight glinted off the auburn highlights in his hair. "Maybe you could."

EIGHT

"Nervous?" Will asked Andie when they were nearly to Jackson and the hospital later that afternoon.

"A little," she admitted.

He wanted to reach across the Jeep and grip her hand, to offer her whatever comfort he could. But he didn't dare. Not with Emily watching them so carefully from the backseat, as she'd been doing since they picked her up from the Lazy Jake an hour earlier.

"I'll be there with you," he said in an undertone. "Don't know if that helps any, but you could pinch me if you start feeling down."

She laughed and lightly pinched the skin of his forearm. "I feel much better now. Thanks."

Despite her studied casualness, he couldn't help but wonder how she was really handling the emotional turmoil of the new baby. He knew it couldn't be easy on her, not after she'd lost three children of her own. He just didn't believe she was as calm as she seemed.

Still, she had seemed fine that morning when she'd again stirred to life in his embrace. A hell of a lot better than fine. Heavenly. She had been soft and responsive, her body flushed with passion and little cries of ecstasy filling her bedroom as he entered her, as he drowned in her arms.

The sound of her pleasure echoed in his mind, and Will felt his blood churn through him, felt his pulse kick up a notch just from remembering it. She'd been all heat and fire in his arms, responsive and arousing.

He blew out a breath and forced the desire away by concentrating on the serpentine two-lane road to Jackson.

They'd left much later than he'd planned, simply because he hadn't possessed the strength to drag himself out of her arms. He'd found a sweet haven there, one he was loathe to leave.

When he was with her, with her surrounding him, engulfing him, nothing else existed. Not the past, not the future. Just Andie, with her crooked smile and her gentle, giving nature and her lithe, welcoming body.

He probably would have stayed there all day if the chickens hadn't started a hungry ruckus close to noon that sent Andie, barefoot and dressed only in her robe, rushing outside in a flurry of guilt to feed them.

He chuckled, remembering it, which earned him quizzical looks from both the females in his vehicle.

"When are we gonna be there, Dad?" Emily emerged from her headphones to ask the eternal question.

"A few more minutes, Em."

She subsided back into whatever music she was listening to, and he sighed. One step forward, two steps back. That's how he felt dealing with his daughter. He'd start making a little progress with her, then something would set her off and she would withdraw to a place he couldn't reach.

When they'd picked her up at the Lazy Jake around one, she'd stared at Andie suspiciously. "What's she doing here?" Emily had asked, her tone bordering on rudeness. "And why do I have to sit in the back?"

He'd reined in his temper. "She's coming with us to the hospital. You'll have more room back there, anyway."

When Emily had opened her mouth to argue, Andie swiftly defused the situation. She'd kept up a subtle diversionary tactic, asking Em about the softball game the day before, about her Lazy Jake friends and the classes that would be starting the next day.

It hadn't taken long for Em to begin to thaw. By the time they reached the outskirts of Whiskey Creek, she had forgotten most of her pique.

She'd even laughed at a story Andie told about taking her goat to the preschool one day and all the children's efforts to keep Mr. Whiskers from eating the carpet. The sound of her own laughter seemed to take Emily aback, though, and she'd quickly withdrawn to her headphones and the teen magazine she'd picked up in Whiskey Creek.

His daughter was reading teen magazines. When the hell had that happened? Seemed like only yesterday she was just the size of Beth's new little one.

He didn't have time to brood about it, though, because the farm and rangeland were giving way to the expensive homes on the outskirts of Jackson, and the traffic around them was picking up.

"It's about time!" a radiant Beth groused when

they walked into the hospital room a short time later. "What took you guys so long?"

For an instant, Will pictured tangled sheets and sweet oblivion. Something of his thoughts must have shown on his face, because when he glanced behind him at Andie, she blushed crimson and took great interest in a picture hanging on the wall.

He couldn't suppress a slow, pleased grin. "Good to see you, too, brat," he teased, suddenly feeling better about life than he had in a long time. "Where's the new little rugrat?"

She took mock offense, even as she studied him closely, as if he'd just sprouted a pair of horns. "His name is Dustin Jace Walker. And he's beautiful."

"I hope he's cuter than you were at his age. I never saw an uglier runt in my life than you the day the folks brought you home from the hospital. Red and scrunched up and ornery all the time."

"I grew out of it. Too bad you never did," she retorted, but her eyes filled with moisture as she looked at him.

What was the matter? he wondered. Hadn't she ever seen him smile and joke before? Had he been so wrapped up in his own problems that he hadn't taken the time to tease his little sister? He cleared his throat and kissed the top of her head. "I'm proud of you, sis."

"Thanks. Same goes," she whispered, then glanced at Emily and Andie waiting in the doorway. "Hi, you two. What'd you bring me?"

Her blush fading to a delightful pink tinge, Andie laughed and walked to the bed. "No kid, no presents. Cough him over, hon."

"You'll have to wait a minute. Sorry. Jace took him

to the nursery for a diaper change. We could have done it here, but all the nurses like to make a fuss over him."

"Jace or the baby?" Andie asked.

"Both, I think." Beth grinned. "There's something about a big, rough cowboy holding his baby that just tugs at a woman's heart."

She gestured to Emily. "Hi there. You have any hugs for your old aunt Beth?"

Emily looked torn, her sweep of brown hair dipping into her eyes, then she solemnly, quickly, hugged her aunt. She stepped away just as Jace came in carrying the baby.

"Okay, pal," Will said, only half-joking. "What's to stop me from beating the hell out of you right now for going off into the hills and leaving my pregnant sister alone all day yesterday?"

His brother-in-law winced but held up the baby, bundled in a receiving blanket. "You wouldn't slug a guy holding a brand-new baby, would you, Tanner?"

Will frowned. "Give him back to his mother, and you and I can just take a walk out into the parking lot. I might forgive you after I've bashed your face into a few cars."

Jace—one of the few men in the world Will could truly call his friend—just laughed and clapped him on the shoulder. "Wouldn't be a fair fight. You're a half-head bigger than me and a hundred times meaner."

"Yeah, but you're uglier. I'd say that just about makes us even."

"Okay, you two. Break it up." Andie stepped forward. "Jace, you've had him long enough. Let me see this little sweetheart."

All his big-brother posturing pushed aside, Will watched Andie take the child. His chest tightened as he saw the gentle way she held the baby and the smile that even reached her eyes, washing away the lingering shadows in their jade depths.

"Hi there," she whispered, and rubbed her cheek against the baby. "Oh, you are a handsome one. Beth, he's perfect. Didn't I tell you he'd be worth all the pain you went through?"

"Ha. Pain? What pain?"

Andie smiled. "They must have you on some heavy-duty drugs." She cuddled the baby for several more minutes, then turned to Emily. "How'd you like to hold your new cousin?"

Emily, perched on one of the two chairs in the room, looked at the child with a mixture of trepidation and intrigue on her face, then she shrugged and held out her arms.

"He's tiny," she whispered after Andie gingerly handed her the bundled-up baby. She pulled the blanket aside and stroked a miniature foot, then put her finger against his curled-up hand. He instinctively gripped it, and Emily flashed a quick, wide smile. "Look at that! He's holding my hand."

She looked so damn much like her mother, Will thought. Same grin. Same little turned-up nose. He felt around for the familiar crushing guilt that usually accompanied the thought of Sarah, but today all he could find was a dull ache. He didn't have time to dwell on the reasons why that might be, because Emily was handing his new nephew to him.

Almost as soon as he took the fragile weight in his

arms, the baby closed his milky blue eyes and fell asleep.

Jace grinned. "Beth, looks like we found a handy baby-sitter."

Will smiled wryly and laid Dustin back in his bassinet. "Not anytime soon, pal. Maybe in about sixteen or seventeen years. Who knows, I might even have decided to forgive you by then for putting me through yesterday."

"Guys," Andie interjected, again the peacemaker, "I think we better let Beth open some of these presents before she breaks her neck trying to see what's inside."

"Good idea." Beth grinned and reached for the top one. It didn't take her long to open the gifts, first the tiny sailor suit they had picked out from the little store in Whiskey Creek before they got Emily, then a new robe and some fancy bottles of lotions from Andie.

Beth held up the last gift. "One more, Jace. Do you want to open it?"

"I wouldn't want to spoil your fun, sweetheart," he drawled.

Beth made a face at her husband but enthusiastically ripped open the package. From his angle, Will couldn't see what was in it, but he watched his sister's features soften. She pulled the gift reverently from the wrappings, and Will felt a shock of recognition go through him. The baby blanket. Andie had given it to Beth after all.

He shot a quick, searching glance at her, sitting in the chair next to him. She was biting her bottom lip, concentrating on the walls, the floor, on anything but the blanket. He could feel her pain tugging at him, as taut and strong as a lariat between them. Spurred only by the need to comfort her, he reached a hand out and rested it on the fist she had tightly clenched on her thigh. She managed a wobbly smile, turning her hand over and squeezing his fingers so tightly it nearly hurt.

"It's gorgeous!" Beth held it up so Jace could see. "Look at those colors! Did you make it yourself, Andie?"

"A long time ago," she answered quietly.

Beth glanced up, then stared at their joined hands. Her expression grew thoughtful as she looked first at him, then at Andie. He could practically see the wheels spinning in her head, but she said nothing, just watched them carefully for the rest of the hour they visited.

They would have talked longer, but right in the middle of the conversation, Beth yawned. Will immediately stood up.

"Ladies, it looks like we'd better let the new mama get some rest," he said.

"Just one more look," Andie said. She leaned over the sleeping baby and traced the back of her fingers down his cheek. "You be good for your mama now," she ordered, then followed Emily out the door.

The hard blue of the September Wyoming sky assaulted them as they walked through the automatic doors of the hospital. Emily walked several paces ahead of him and Andie, as if she didn't want to be seen with them.

Definitely no progress today, he thought.

In the old days he and Emily used to have a Sunday afternoon tradition, he remembered. It was their special time together, just the two of them, usually the only chance he had during his hectic schedule to be with her. They would leave Sarah at home and he would take Emily on some outing, to a baseball game or the zoo or just for a bike ride around the neighborhood. Wherever their mood carried them. He had treasured those times as much as she had, had relished the rare opportunity to be with her, since his job usually kept him so occupied.

How many Sundays had gone by since he'd broken the tradition? A dozen? A hundred?

Three years worth, he realized. Guilt and regret washed through him at the thought of how much he'd missed. He'd stood by and done nothing while his daughter slipped away from him, inch by inch. And he wanted her back, dammit. With a fierce ache, he wanted to return to the days when she looked at him as if she thought he could do anything in the world.

Starting now. He stopped walking so abruptly, Andie stopped with him.

"What's the matter?" she asked.

"Do you have anywhere you need to be?"

She shook her head. "I planned to do a little gardening, but it can wait until tomorrow. Why? What did you have in mind?"

He watched his daughter, who by now had reached the Jeep and was leaning against it, her arms crossed, her expression impatient. Andie followed his gaze to the girl, wondering what she could do to break through Emily's hard shell. His daughter obviously didn't like her. Andie didn't know why that should hurt so much, but it did.

"I was just thinking," Will said, "that I wouldn't mind showing Emily around Jackson a little. I don't think she's ever been in town and I'd hate for her to miss seeing a real live Wild West tourist trap."

Andie laughed as they reached his Jeep. "Sounds fun. What do you think, Emily?"

"About what?"

"Your dad thought you might like to spend some time here in Jackson Hole. Feel like a little shopping?"

"My dad hates shopping."

"All men do," Andie confided. "Isn't that just about the saddest thing you've ever heard? Can you imagine hating shopping?"

Emily relaxed and even uttered a little giggle. Andie smiled back and threw a conspiratorial arm around her shoulders. "What do you say we make your dad miserable all day long and take him to every single store in town?"

He groaned, which set Emily giggling all the more. "Cool. Especially clothes stores. He really hates those."

"You bet," Andie promised. "Believe me, Jackson has tons of clothes stores."

And maybe a few hours of shopping, she mused, would be just what she needed to take her mind off of the residue of pain in her heart.

"How's she doing back there?"

Andie glanced in the backseat, where Emily was curled up in the corner using her wadded-up jacket for a pillow. Her hair was in her eyes, and Andie battled a powerful urge to reach back and brush it away.

"Asleep. Didn't take her long, did it?"

"It never does." Will flashed a smile and reached

for her hand. At the feel of his strong fingers against hers, their first real contact since the hospital, Andie leaned her head back and closed her eyes, contentment washing through her. She couldn't imagine one single thing more wonderful than this, heading home through the dark with Will beside her while a soft jazz melody eased out of the speakers.

"You ought to get some rest too," he said, his voice just a low murmur.

She shook her head. She didn't want it to end yet. The day had been too precious, a revelation, and she wanted to treasure every single moment of it.

They hadn't made it to every store in town. Just most of them. While they walked up and down the wooden boardwalks of the funky tourist town, she had discovered a completely different side of Will. Gone was the gruff demeanor that usually encased him. In its place was a man who obligingly followed her and Emily from shop to shop, teasing and joking and even laughing aloud with growing frequency as the day wore on.

She also discovered the seductive joy in being part of a family, even if she had to keep reminding herself it was only for a little while.

At the first store they stopped at, she bought one of those disposable cameras. But even without the pictures she took throughout the day, she knew her own snapshots of their time together would be imprinted in her mind forever: Will, red-faced, gulping a big glass of water after scooping a tortilla chip into the extra-hot salsa at the outdoor Mexican café they'd stopped at. Father and daughter looking up in awe at the famous arch of entwined elk antlers in the town square.

She and Emily thrusting their faces through a wooden cutout of saloon girls and laughing uproariously as Will spent five minutes trying to figure out how the camera worked.

They mostly window-shopped, but Andie and Emily both picked out the same pair of earrings, burnished brass cowboys atop bucking broncs. She found a pasta cookbook she'd been looking for, and Will gave in and peeled out his wallet when Emily fell in love with a stuffed grizzly bear.

He was so good-natured about the whole day that Andie rewarded him with a T-shirt sporting a goofy-looking moose decked out in fancy red sunglasses that she'd bought in one store when he wasn't looking. He seemed ridiculously pleased with it and promised to wear it as soon as possible.

She smiled at the memory, a smile that ended in a wide yawn. Will must have seen it because he squeezed her fingers.

"Get some rest," he repeated.

She fought it for a few more minutes, but the steady movement of the vehicle through the night relaxed her, and a sweet lassitude spread from her shoulders to her toes. Her last thought before falling asleep was that underneath his gruff facade, Will Tanner was actually a nice man.

The motion of the Jeep had stopped when she finally slipped out of sleep. The engine still purred, but they were no longer moving.

Disoriented, she shook her head to clear it and realized her cheek was pressed against his shoulder, his arm cradling her next to his hard warmth. His cotton shirt was soft against her skin, and the smell of him—cedary and male—filled her senses.

She closed her eyes again, loath to leave the refuge of his arms, but she forced herself to pull away.

"Sorry," she murmured.

He smiled. "I enjoyed it," he said. "You don't even talk in your sleep. Much."

She glanced out the window and saw the familiar shape of the Limber Pine ranch house. For the first time that she could recall, she didn't feel the usual burst of relief at being home, the welcoming sense of peace she experienced just pulling into the driveway. All that waited for her here was an empty bed, with sheets that probably still carried the scent of him.

"I'll walk you to your door," he said.

"You don't have to."

"Never let it be said that Annabel Tanner's son didn't learn the proper way to end an evening with his lady companion."

"Dear me, no!" she said, smiling.

He opened her door for her, and they walked quietly across the driveway and up the steps to her back door.

"Thank you, Will," she said softly, one hand on the doorknob. "For letting me spend the day with you and Em. I enjoyed it."

"You were very good with her."

"She's a sweet girl."

He snorted. "Right."

"She is," Andie insisted. "She's just afraid right now, and I don't think she knows how to express that fear."

"Of what? What does an eleven-year-old girl have to be afraid of?"

She paused. *Stay out of it. It's not your business,* a warning voice told her. But the instinct to help him, to at least take some steps to heal the gulf between father and daughter, was much stronger.

"Of being alone," she finally said. "Of you leaving her."

"That's crazy!" he snapped. "She knows I'd never go anywhere without her."

"Will, she's a little girl who lost her mother in a terrible way. Just when she was probably coming to terms with that, you had to go and nearly get yourself killed. How is she supposed to feel? I sense a lot of anger in her, and I think she's trying so hard to grow up fast—to be independent—so she can show you she doesn't need you."

He opened his mouth as if to argue with her, then blew out a breath in a huff. "You know, it makes a strange sort of sense. She started acting up right around the time I was shot."

"And she probably started pulling away from you then too."

He nodded. "So how do I convince her I'm not going to leave?"

"Just do what you did today. Spend time with her. Don't shut her out of your life. She strikes me as a pretty smart girl, and I think if you sat down with her and talked out what you've both been going through, you might be able to make some progress at working past it."

"Talk to her. Why didn't I think of that?" He grinned. "You know, it just might work."

"Try it."

"How'd you get to be so smart?"

She simply didn't possess the strength to resist that smile, the one that made him look so much younger, that softened the harsh planes of his face. "Years and years of practice," she replied, and smiled back when he reached for her and drew her against his body.

Still smiling, she settled there as if she belonged nowhere else, as if she had been made to be molded against him, and lifted her face willingly for his kiss. A sigh whispered out of her, and she closed her eyes just as he touched his lips to hers.

He tasted like chocolate, she thought, probably from the ice-cream cones they'd shared just before leaving Jackson. Sweet, rich chocolate. She tasted it on her tongue, on her lips, and knew she'd never be able to eat ice cream again without thinking of this moment.

Everything suddenly seemed so intense to her: The wind carrying the scent of pine and flowers had never smelled so sweet. The barn owl's call had never sounded so appealing. His hair between her fingertips had never felt so silky.

He licked at the corner of her lips, and she opened for him as the heady taste of chocolate grew stronger. She dipped her tongue into his mouth for a better taste, and he groaned and pulled her closer still. Yes, she could definitely stay here forever, right here in his arms—

"Stop it. Just stop it!"

They jerked apart at Emily's shocked voice, as if their roles were reversed and they were two teenagers caught by their fathers. Flushing, Andie scrambled away from Will. How could they possibly have forgotten his daughter, asleep just a few feet away?

The girl stood outside the Jeep, her fists clenched as she glared at them through eyes that still held traces of sleep.

"Emily—" Andie began.

"You can't take her place. You can't. You *can't*!" She started to cry and slammed the car door shut, then raced into the cottage.

"Emily!" Will walked down the steps toward her, then turned back to Andie, as if he couldn't decide what to do.

"Go to her, Will," Andie said. She drew a shaky breath, wondering how much more tumult her poor, battered emotions could handle.

It was palpable, this withdrawal of his. At the very mention of his dead wife, he had stiffened and pulled away from Andie as if he couldn't bear to touch her. As if their closeness of that day and the night before was nothing more than a brief and very regrettable weakness.

"Go to her," she repeated. "She needs you now."

"I'm sorry, Andie," he said, his voice hoarse, then he turned and followed his daughter into the cottage, leaving her alone.

"Me too, Will," she whispered. "Me too."

NINE

"He's growing, isn't he?" Andie hefted Dustin into her arms and nuzzled his soft neck. He smelled of baby powder and that indefinable, irresistible scent of an infant's skin.

"Three weeks old today," Beth said proudly. "Can you believe it?"

Three weeks? It felt like a lifetime since she'd helped bring the baby into the world. Since the night she'd confronted her own pain. Since she'd awakened in Will's arms.

She'd barely seen him since Emily caught them in each other's arms that night after their trip to Jackson. When she did, he was back to his former gruff self and so evasive, she'd stopped trying to reach him.

In truth, she'd hardly had time the past three weeks to worry about Will. Between all the harvesting of her garden and the canning and the endless preparations it took to ready the ranch for the coming winter, she had more than she could handle.

It was only late at night, while the autumn wind

sent leaves scuttling against the windows, that she wondered if she'd imagined the whole thing, somehow conjured up their shattering intimacy in some wild, delusional corner of her mind.

Yet when she closed her eyes, she could still feel the imprint of his hands on her skin, still taste his mouth against hers, still feel him filling her, consuming her.

"Andie?"

Beth's questioning voice dragged Andie from her thoughts, and she blushed, hot color soaking her cheeks. "Sorry. What did you say?"

"I said Dustin already seems less of a baby and more like a little boy."

Andie forced a smile and looked at the baby's tiny features. "Yep. He'll be graduating from college before you know it."

Beth chuckled and settled deeper into the chair in Andie's office at the school. "I'm so glad I stopped by. I need you for perspective in my life."

"How are you really doing?" Andie asked.

Her friend gave a radiant smile. "Better than I've ever been. It's hectic and exhausting, especially with this colic, and I don't get more than two hours of sleep at a time, but I had no idea it would be so exhilarating. How about you? Are you still functioning without me around here?"

Andie laughed. "Just barely. It helps that the classes are becoming smaller since many of the workers have moved on. The big summer crunch is over and most of them are heading into Idaho for the potato crop or up to the fruit crops in Oregon and Washington."

"Well, I'm ready to come back whenever you say the word."

"Take all the time you need. You know the job is yours whether you come back next month or next year. Somehow we'll manage to get by without you."

Beth laughed just as a noise sounded from the doorway. They both looked up to find Emily there, clutching the book she'd been reading in the playroom.

"Aunt Beth, can I walk down to the grocery store for a drink?" she asked, studiously avoiding even looking at Andie. It hurt, Andie admitted. She thought they had become friends during the shopping trip to Jackson. A quick image of them laughing together at Will as he tried on hats at an old-fashioned milliner's shop in town flashed through her mind, and she sighed. Whatever warmth had been between them that day had dried up as surely as Miller's Creek in the heat of the summer.

Oblivious to the undercurrents, Beth smiled at her niece. "Sure, hon. Let me find my purse and I'll give you a dollar."

"I've got money," Emily muttered.

"Here." Beth fumbled in the pocket of the diaper bag and triumphantly pulled out a few wadded-up bills. She handed them to Emily. "Why don't you get us a couple of sodas while you're over there?"

Emily's mouth, so much like her father's, tightened into a thin line. "I'll get you one, Aunt Beth. *She* can find her own." Her brown curls swinging, she turned and marched out the door, leaving Beth staring openmouthed after her.

Dustin let out a squawk, and Andie realized she

was holding him too tightly. She relaxed her arms. "Sorry, sweetheart," she whispered, kissing the downy skin of his forehead.

"All right," Beth said. "What's going on?"

Andie sighed again. "Your niece doesn't much like me. I think she's afraid I have designs on her father."

"What on earth gave her that idea?"

Andie blushed again as she pictured her and Will entwined in each other's arms, oblivious to the world. "I haven't any idea," she lied.

"Well, do you? Have designs on her father, I mean?"

"I wouldn't get very far, even if I did," she mumbled. Will obviously regretted their closeness. His daughter's accusing words about how Andie couldn't take her mother's place seemed to have jerked him back to reality. If he wanted to climb right back inside his grim existence, how could she stop him?

"He's miserable, you know."

Andie glanced up from the gurgling baby. "Who? Will?"

"Yes. That stubborn brother of mine. I don't know what's gotten into him, but ever since Dustin was born, it seems like he can't work hard enough. He's either putting in double shifts at the jail or spending all his time with Jace rounding up strays for the winter. It's almost like he's running from something."

She sent a speculative look Andie's way. "Or maybe *someone*."

Andie evaded her friend's gaze. "Maybe one of these days he'll slow his running down long enough to turn around and see that *someone* has no intention of trying to catch him."

"You'd be the best thing to ever happen to both Will and Emily," Beth said solemnly. "They need softness and laughter in their lives again. Will needs you, whether he wants to admit it or not."

A piercing ache spread through her, a powerful, sharp yearning to heal him, to make him laugh, and to tuck both him and his daughter against her heart.

To be needed. It was her fatal flaw, she thought, that overwhelming hunger to be needed.

Still, in the scheme of things, what she wanted didn't much matter. Will would be gone in a few weeks, anyway, just another part of the endless cycle of autumn migration in Whiskey Creek: the raptors and waterfowl catching a ride on the jetstream south; the workers and their families moving on to greener crops.

And Will, returning to the desert of his grief.

The sun straddled the mountains to the west, sending long, stretched-out shadows across the terrain when Will climbed out of the Jeep at the Limber Pine that evening.

The dogs barked a greeting and rushed to him from their favorite resting spot underneath the willow tree, as if it had been months since they'd seen him instead of just that morning. He cracked a smile and gave them the requisite pats. The two big retrievers fussed over him like this whenever he returned to the Limber Pine at the end of the day. Maybe that was why he always felt that little spurt of anticipation when he pulled into the driveway of the ranch. He always felt . . . welcomed, somehow.

Like coming home.

The thought appeared out of nowhere, and he jerked upright. Where the hell had that come from? His home was in Phoenix. He had a job to do there and that was where he damn well would stay, not on some dinky ranch in a backwater Wyoming town.

So what if he had a couple of dogs licking his hands and careening around his legs every time he came here? Phoenix—and unfinished business—waited for him. He'd do well to keep that uppermost in his mind.

A gust of wind sent leaf skeletons skittering across the lawn, then whirled them down the road. In a matter of weeks, he'd be just like those leaves, Will reminded himself, blowing out of there without once looking back.

He gave the dogs one last pat and was opening the screen door to the cottage when a flash of color near the front porch of the ranch house caught his eye.

Andie, in a bright yellow sweatshirt and faded jeans, knelt by her flower bed, yanking flowers from the soil. The dying sun glinted off her dark hair, and she looked as fresh and appealing as a sunflower. Hungry desire kicked through him at the sight of her. He curled his fingers on the door handle, willing it away.

He'd do well to remember what Emily had shouted that night three weeks ago. *You can't take her place. You can't.*

At her words, he had felt as if he'd been doused in frigid runoff, and Sarah's face, silently accusing, had burned into his mind. How could he have forgotten? How could he have let the undeniable magic he found in Andie's arms distract him from the cause that had kept him going for the past three years? Vengeance. If he wanted to save his soul, he had to run Zamora to ground. He owed it to Sarah and he owed it to himself. Maybe then the demons of guilt would slither away, and he could find peace.

You found peace, a voice in his head reminded him. For an instant, he saw himself and Andie in her garden, bodies and spirits entangled, and he had to force himself to breathe.

Andie must have seen him drive up because she paused for a moment as their gazes met, then lifted a gloved hand in a polite wave. For an instant, he considered fleeing inside and locking the door behind him, away from the sight and the scent and the overwhelming temptation of her. But if he'd learned anything these past three weeks as he tried to put as much distance between them as he could, he'd learned running didn't help. No matter how hard he worked, how many steers he chased, how much paperwork he filled out at the jail, he couldn't escape her. He couldn't keep from remembering how she'd looked in the moonlight, her skin flushed with passion, her eyes glittering with need. And how damn *right* she'd felt in his arms.

He would just say hello, he thought. It was the neighborly thing to do, after all. Just say hello and keep his promise to tell her what was happening with Jessop.

He thought he saw a glittering awareness shiver through her eyes as he walked closer, but the temperature of her smile just about matched the arctic wind that would be blowing down out of the mountains in a few weeks.

She climbed to her feet. "Sheriff."

"Looks like you've been hard at work." He gestured to the wheelbarrow piled high with plants.

"I'm just cleaning up a bit. Clearing the annuals out for the winter. After that frost we had the other night, most of them are finished blooming anyway."

"Sounds fun."

She grimaced. "I hate this part of gardening, when the flowers have begun to wither and the harvest is nearly over. It's so grim. So final. I know I have to do it, but I just hate it. It's like finally admitting summer's over."

She had a smudge of dirt edging her cheekbone, he noticed. Before he had time to think it through, he stepped forward and rubbed his thumb over the spot. It was a huge mistake. A monumental mistake. At the feel of her velvety skin, he froze, his chest suddenly tight, his blood pumping sluggishly through his veins.

Their gazes met and locked, and he watched the black of her pupils expand, leaving only a thin, gold-flecked circle of green. She drew in a gasping breath, and it was enough to jerk him back to his senses. He stepped away as quickly as if he'd just wrapped his fingers around a prickly pear.

"Sorry. You . . . uh . . . you left some dirt on your cheek there."

She rubbed the sleeve of her sweatshirt over the spot so vigorously, he was afraid she would scour the skin away.

"Where's Emily tonight?" she asked, avoiding his gaze as she carted another load of uprooted plants to the wheelbarrow.

"Beth got some bee in her bonnet about having Emily stay at the Bar W for the night. Jace had to go to some cattle sale in Laramie, I guess, and Beth suddenly decided she wanted company."

Andie sent him a quick look. "When was this?"

"She called me an hour ago. Why?"

Andie flexed her jaw, as if she was either trying not to laugh or not to scream about something. "No reason. Just curious."

"Anyway," he continued, "I've been meaning to tell you what happened with Jessop, but I haven't been around much."

"I noticed." She yanked off her leather work gloves with a bit more force than necessary and shoved them in her back pocket.

That damn guilt coursed through him again. Here was another one of the things he'd screwed up in his life. He'd used her. Selfishly, heedlessly used her at a time when she'd been at her most emotionally vulnerable.

He glanced away. "Yesterday I cited him for renting out unsafe and unsanitary housing. Under a deal made with the county attorney, if he builds new quarters for his workers, they'll drop the charges and the fines. He's agreed to bring in temporary trailers in the meantime. He's not about it, but I think he knows he doesn't have any kind of choice."

The cool reserve surrounding her dissolved as a wide, pleased smile lit up her face, sending his insides tumbling around. "That's terrific, Will! Thank you so much!"

He cleared his throat. "You're welcome."

"I mean it. Thank you! You did a good thing, Sheriff. Tom's a bully and most people would rather not cross him. I'm so glad you didn't let that stop you."

He didn't want her gratitude. He wanted . . . he wanted . . . Just what the hell did he want? If he knew the answer to that, maybe he wouldn't be filled with these conflicting urges to both back away from her as fast as he could and grab her so tightly she wouldn't even want to think about getting away.

"I didn't arrest him like you asked me to," he pointed out gruffly.

"Well, sometimes I go a little overboard when something's important to me. I think you did exactly the right thing."

She studied him for a moment as if debating something, then she stepped forward. He nearly pushed her away, but he forced himself to remain as motionless as the mountains around them as she stood right against him. "Thank you, Will," she whispered.

His blood churned as he felt the caressing butterfly dance of her lips against his cheek. The feel of her, the intoxicating scent of lavender that clung to her, sizzled through him. He had thought her effect on him would fade with time, but he ached with the need to touch her, to taste just a little of her softness.

"Andie." Her name was a plea on his lips.

She said nothing, just watched him out of those aspen-leaf eyes that could see straight into his soul. Their gazes locked and held as, against his better judgment, he lowered his head.

Their lips met and clung, hers gentle and tranquil, his rough and desperate. He felt the impact of her kiss rock him, as if she'd dislodged the ground beneath him.

How could they make such a powerful connection with just the contact of mouth on mouth? He had no idea, but it seared through him, potent and strong. He wanted to tuck her against him, to spend the rest of his life right here, with her soft breath blowing between her lips, with her body nestled against him so sweetly.

Gradually he became aware that the sun had slid below the mountain and the air had begun to chill. As the crosswind burrowed cold fingers through his clothing, he jerked back to awareness. To her in his arms. To his hand just inches from exploring her tempting curves.

What the hell was he doing?

He pulled back, his breathing ragged, and looked away, unable to face her. "I'm sorry, Andie. I vowed to myself I wouldn't let that happen again."

"Why?"

He debated coming up with an excuse, anything but the truth. How could he tell her that because of her, he'd spent a night at peace for the first time in three years? That while he was lost in the wonder of making love to her, he'd been able to shake, if only for a little while, the hounds of guilt that pursued him?

And that he felt ashamed and brutally selfish because right then he wanted that oblivion again, with a fierce, all-consuming need.

"I don't have anything left to give you," he finally said. That, at least, was part of the truth.

Her bittersweet half smile nearly broke his heart. "I never once asked you for anything, Will."

"Andie, listen to me. Everything in me died right along with my wife and son. Everything. The only thing I have left is Emily and I'm screwing that up too.

Dammit, Andie, you deserve better than that, than some broken-down excuse for a cop who will never be able to give you any kind of promises."

"I don't need promises," she said, her voice barely a whisper in the night. "I don't need anything. Just you."

He should fight her, he told himself, should turn on his heel and walk into his cottage. But he wasn't strong enough. Everything in him cried out for that connection again, for the peace and solace he found only with her. He groaned even as he reached for her.

Like her ranch, she was warm and welcoming, and she sighed his name as he kissed her.

"You feel so good to me," she whispered. "I've wondered since the other night if I imagined it all."

"Did you?" he asked gruffly, barely able to think.

"No." She trailed a kiss to his throat, to where his pulse throbbed out his desire. "If anything, I left out some pretty darned important information. Like how, when you're kissing me, I light up like the sky above Whiskey Creek on the Fourth of July."

He groaned again. "Much more talk like that, sweetheart, and we're going to end up giving that old goat staked up back there one hell of a show."

She peered around him to where Mr. Whiskers was nibbling the grass along the west fence.

"Corrupting the morals of a goat. Shame on you, Sheriff."

His deep laugh surprised both of them. It rumbled out of him, and she rewarded him with a winsome smile, then grabbed his hand. Somehow they made it inside the house and up the steep wooden stairs, stopping on each one to discard more of their clothing and share another long, drugging kiss.

By the time they reached her bedroom, he was shaking with need. So was she, he realized, and a primitive satisfaction swept through him. She wanted him as badly as he burned for her.

He barely made it to the bed before he had to be inside her. Bodies entwined, they fell onto the soft quilt.

"You feel so good," she repeated as he entered her, and he threw back his head at the sweet, silken depths closing around him, embracing him. Welcoming him.

"Damn right I feel good," he growled. "How'd you know?"

She laughed, and, as always, the sultry, arousing sound rippled down his spine like the caress of her fingers.

"Maybe I'm psychic," she said.

"You're something. I don't know if *psychic* is the word I'd use, but you're definitely something."

"Is it a good something or a bad something?" she asked, then groaned as he pushed deep inside her again.

"Good. Very, very good," he said, then lost himself in the sweet oblivion of her body.

He watched her sleep for a long time, the little soughing breaths she took, the delicate tracery of veins in her eyelids. It would be so hard to leave her. He felt his chest grow tight at the thought of it, yet he also could feel his time there slipping away. Hank had already stopped by the jail that week to tell Will he'd be ready to resume his duties any day now.

He should have been relieved, should have been so eager to return to Phoenix and what waited for him there. But he had to admit that beyond the ache he felt at leaving Andie, a few of his pangs were for the job, for something that had once held about the same attraction to him as sitting on a saguaro cactus. Surprisingly, he'd found himself actually enjoying his time there as sheriff. There was something so *gratifying* about being needed and respected by the people he served.

In Phoenix, he was lucky if his own damn sources remembered his name, but here everybody wanted to stop and chat. He had little boys following him around town with admiration in their eyes, had weather-beaten ranchers stop him in the street to shake his hand and ask him how his shoulder was feeling. Just the other day, Betsy Jacobs had dropped by the jail with an extra strawberry pie she'd baked just because she wanted him to know he was doing a good job.

Will suddenly stiffened at the reminder of his job. Damn. He'd left his cellular phone in his jacket, slung over the passenger seat of the Jeep. He'd gotten in the habit of keeping it close so his deputies could reach him if they had an emergency. They would have no idea he was here, he realized. As loath as he was to leave the haven of Andie's bed, he knew he'd have to go out into the cold to grab the phone.

He had a responsibility to all those good folks who remembered his name and brought him strawberry pie.

Feeling his way in the dark, he slid into his jeans.

He decided not to risk waking Andie up by fumbling around for his shirt and he walked quietly out into the hallway. And smack into some kind of table.

He swore as pain radiated from his stubbed toe, then quickly clamped his lips together. A quick glance back to the darkened bedroom showed Andie hadn't awakened, so Will hobbled down the stairs as quietly as he could.

A cold wind grabbed him by the shoulders and shook him as soon as he walked out the door. He'd forgotten how quickly fall came in the mountains. Seemed like one night you were sleeping with just the screens, the next you have to hurry to find the storm windows.

He grabbed his jacket with the phone in the pocket and walked quickly back to the house. He was just easing open the door when a loud ringing vibrated through the dark house.

He fumbled in the jacket pocket to find his cellular, then punched the talk button before the ringing could wake Andie.

"Yeah?" he said, only to be met by a dial tone and another ring.

Must be her phone. He chuckled wryly and shook his head. All these gadgets that were supposed to make life simpler were sure a hell of a lot of trouble.

By the time he found the kitchen light switch so he could figure out where her phone was, it had rung one more time. He glanced at the daisy clock above her stove. Who would be calling her at eleven-thirty at night?

He picked up the receiver, prepared to give an earful to whoever was on the line. Andie must have already picked up the extension upstairs, though, because someone was already talking.

He started to hang up, not wanting to listen in on her private conversation, but then the words he'd heard registered and he jerked the phone back to his ear.

"I'm coming for you, little schoolteacher," an oddly distorted voice said, chortling. "You knew I would, didn't you? I've told you just what I was going to do to you, and how much you're going to suffer. Won't be long now, and nobody, especially not that stupid new sheriff you like so much, will be able to find what's left of you when I'm done."

TEN

Rage, fierce and hot, swept through Will with the wildness of a wind-whipped brush fire. He listened to the call, to the threats and obscene promises, for a few more shocked seconds. He was just about ready to tell the son of a bitch where to go when he heard a soft click, followed by the buzz of a dial tone.

He slammed the phone down and thundered up the stairs two at a time.

When he shoved open the bedroom door, he found Andie sitting on the bed in her nightgown, her arms folded tightly around herself, staring at the phone as if it had just grown fangs.

"What the hell was that all about?"

She avoided his gaze. "What's what all about?"

"Don't play games with me. That vicious phone call. He's called you before, hasn't he?"

"A few times." She shrugged. "It's just a sicko who gets some weird thrill out of terrorizing people. I'm not going to let it get to me."

"Well, I am. Dammit, Andie. Those things can escalate faster than you can hang up the phone. How long has this been going on?"

"Most—most of the summer," she admitted, and for the first time he realized she was shaking. He crossed the room and pulled her from the bed into his arms, berating himself for yelling at her. That was absolutely the last thing she needed after the vitriol that had just spewed out of her phone.

She felt slight and fragile in his arms. Her hands fluttered at his sides, then gripped his back tightly. He held her for a long time while tiny tremors shook her body, consumed with the need to protect her, to comfort her.

When was the last time he'd felt this way about anyone but Emily? he wondered, as he stroked the delicate curve of her spine, the gossamer silk of her hair.

Whatever he was doing seemed to be working because gradually he felt her shaking slow as she calmed down. Finally she pulled away, her features once again composed, and his lawman's instincts forced their way out.

"I need to ask you some questions, Andie. Do you feel up to it?"

"Will, I really don't want to talk about it." She reached for a robe from the window seat.

"I'm sorry, sweetheart, but I need to know a few things so we can catch the guy. I'll try to make it short."

She nodded. "Okay. Go ahead."

"How often does he call?"

"It . . . it depends." Her voice faltered, then grew stronger. "Sometimes a few nights in a row, sometimes a week apart. There doesn't seem to be any kind of pattern."

"Have all the calls been more of the same?"

"I don't know. He seems to be getting worse." Her hands tightened on the lapels of her robe. "He's never made such blatant threats before. It's always been sort of vague."

Will muttered a long string of oaths. It definitely sounded like the guy's fixation was escalating. "Have you seen anybody suspicious in the area? Do you have any enemies, anybody you've pissed off in the last few weeks?"

They stared at each other. He could read the same realization dawning in her eyes that had just occurred to him. "Jessop," he growled. "It has to be Jessop."

Was it? Andie couldn't say for sure. The drawl was the same, but most of the men in the county had the same speech cadence. Whoever it was had disguised his voice so much she just didn't know.

"Remember his threats at the softball game?" Will continued. "He didn't sound like he was messing around. It has to be him."

Andie felt a chill sweep over her again.

"We'll put a tracer on the phone," Will went on, "and add extra patrols near the house and the school. Until we catch him, under no circumstances will you be on your own. You'll have to have somebody with you at all times."

How did he do it, she wondered, switch so abruptly from caring and gentle lover to rough and alert soldier?

"No, I won't," she said.

"Yes. You will." He looked startled but unwavering. "Don't argue with me on this, Andie."

"I'm not so sure it's Jessop. But even if it is—really, whoever it is—he's just talking big, trying to scare me off."

"Yeah, well, we can't know that for sure, can we?"

"I am not going to hide this time."

"What do you mean, 'this time'?"

She cinched the tie tightly on her robe. "I ran away once, like a spoiled little girl, when life didn't go the way I wanted it to. I thought I could escape the failure of my marriage, but I learned after I came here that you have to confront your problems or they will dog you for the rest of your life. I refuse to hide again!"

"And I refuse to let anything happen to you. Argue all you want, lady, but I'm going to be on you like mean on a rattler."

"I'm a grown woman who can take care of herself. You don't have anything to say about it."

"Wrong. I'm still the sheriff around here, at least for a few more weeks. Besides that minor little detail, this"—he gestured at the bed—"and what we have together gives me the right to do whatever the hell it takes to keep you safe."

She opened her mouth to argue with him, to make some scathing observation about how he wasn't her father or her brother or her husband.

Just her lover.

But as she looked at him, his brown hair mussed, a worried furrow between his gray wolf eyes, that beautiful mouth tight with concern, she couldn't form the words. They choked in her throat as she stared at him.

He was more than that. So much more. The truth

of it swept over her, engulfing her like a tsunami, and she could do nothing but stand there, her bare feet cold on the hardwood floor of her bedroom.

She loved him.

It burned within her, fierce and strong and so clear, she wondered how she possibly could have missed it. All this time when she'd thought she just wanted to heal him, to bring a little laughter to him, she had been fooling herself. He had been the healer here, had filled the empty, cold place inside her.

How on earth could she have let it happen?

Since coming to Whiskey Creek, she had been guarding her heart so closely, resolute in her solitude. She'd let a few people into her life—Beth, Carly, the children at the center. But never anyone who had the power to devastate her again. And now Will had slipped inside when she wasn't looking with that rare crooked smile and his wounded eyes.

She loved him.

And he was leaving, just as soon as he could shake the Wyoming dirt from his boots.

"Andie? Sweetheart?"

The worry in his voice dragged her back to the reality of the moment. To her bedroom and the cold wood beneath her feet. To the sudden icy coldness in her heart.

"I—I'm sorry. What did you say?"

"I'm going to keep Emily at the Bar W until this thing cools down so she'll be safe and out of the way. I'll move a few of my things over here and sleep on the couch until we catch this guy. I will not let him hurt you."

His words—spoken with all the intensity of a sacred vow—barely registered. The shock of realizing how she felt about him crowded everything else out.

The wise course, the prudent one, would be for her to pull away from him. As it was, she would be shattered when he left. Maybe by drawing her defenses tightly around her now, she could keep from being completely destroyed.

But she was very much afraid it was too late.

Five days later, Will had lost much of his optimism that this would be a quick, easy collar. He had round-the-clock watches at both Andie's and Jessop's ranches, but so far they'd unearthed absolutely nothing out of the ordinary.

If something didn't go down soon, he'd have to reduce the patrols near the Limber Pine, as much as he hated the idea. He just didn't have the manpower in a four-deputy department for this constant watch on Andie.

At least the official patrols would have to be reduced, he amended. With the frighteningly effective grapevine in Whiskey Creek, word must have gotten around that Andie was in danger. All week Shirley had been taking calls at the station house from ranchers offering to help watch the place. Chase Samuelson had offered every one of his ranch hands if Will needed them, and even his grandfather, Jake—eighty if he was a day—had volunteered to take a shift.

If it hadn't been so frustrating to all his instincts as a lawman, he would have found it touching that everybody in town wanted to take care of her. Heartwarming. But with every person who called, his anxiety level accelerated. If word made it to Jessop about the increased vigilance—and there was no question it was only a matter of time until it would—they would probably never catch the bastard.

Summer seemed to have blown away with the first of October, Will thought as he drove through the drizzling rain to the Limber Pine. Already he could see a sprinkling of snow dusting the mountains. Here in the valley, real snow was probably a month or more away, but the nights regularly reached nearly to freezing.

He parked in front of the ranch house and got out. Joey Whitehorse stepped from the shadows on the porch as he approached. His deputy pulled the brim of his Stetson down against the elements.

"It's been real slow, Sheriff," he said. "Only one call—your sister."

"What are you doing out here in the cold, Joe? I hope you haven't been here all afternoon. You can keep watch just as well from inside."

Joey cleared his throat. "I, uh, told Miz McPhee I needed a smoke."

"I didn't know you smoked, Joe."

His deputy shook his head and looked shamefaced in the dim light. "I don't, sir. I just needed a break and that was the only excuse I could think of. I swear that woman's worse than a drill sergeant. Before it started to rain, she made me haul rocks in her garden, shovel out the chicken coop, and stack what felt like a whole winter's worth of firewood. Said as long as I was wastin' my time baby-sittin' her, she'd get some work out of me. I thought I'd get a rest when the sun went down and it started to rain, but she just put me to work inside. Making spaghetti sauce, of all the fool things."

Will chuckled. "At least you can't say it was just another boring stakeout."

"I don't know how much more of this I can take, sir," Joe said emphatically. "I sure hope we catch this guy soon."

"So do I, Joe."

He started up the steps when his deputy called after him. "Hope you don't mind me saying, sir, but Miz McPhee doesn't seem too happy about all this."

"That's too damn bad," Will replied.

Joe grinned. "Yeah, that's what I figured you'd say. Still, you might want to take up smokin', too, so you can stay out of her way. Miz McPhee's bein' pretty easygoin' about us being here, but I don't think it's gonna last long, and she's got one heck of a temper when she's riled."

"Really?" Will asked, intrigued. "When have you ever seen her temper?"

His deputy looked discomfited. "I didn't see it, just heard about it," he mumbled.

"About what, Joe?"

The younger man shoved his hands into the pockets of his coat. "You know my little sister Janice?"

Will vaguely recalled a pretty teenager with shy dark eyes and a sweet smile. "Yeah, I think I met her once at R.J.'s Café."

"Well, she told me about it. One day after school last spring, a few of the older boys were givin' her a hard time. Callin' her squaw and stuff like that. Fact, one of 'em was Jessop's boy, Marty. Guess it's true what they say about the fruit not fallin' far from the tree."

Joey paused. "Anyway, things started gettin' ugly, and I don't know what might have happened if Miz McPhee hadn't been drivin' by. Janice was bawlin', tryin' to walk faster, and these three boys just kept goin' after her and wouldn't let up. Miz McPhee, she stopped that big truck of hers right there in the middle of the road and jumped out and started yellin' to beat the band. Getting right in their faces even though she's such a little thing and these were big cowboys. She told 'em, shame on them for picking on somebody smaller than they were, that it was a cowardly thing to do, and that if she ever so much as heard a whisper about 'em doin' it again, she was gonna horsewhip the lot of 'em."

At the idea of her taking on a bunch of burly young men, a warmth uncoiled inside Will, and he wanted to shake her and kiss her senseless for doing something so foolishly, stupidly brave.

"Well, I guess I'd best head home, sir," Joey said, heading for his patrol car.

"Get some rest, why don't you?" Will called after him.

He stood outside while the rain coated his clothing with a fine mist and watched his deputy drive down the road, then he walked into the ranch house without bothering to knock. If he did, she probably wouldn't let him in, she was so put out by this whole investigation, he thought, chuckling.

Andie must have started a fire in the living room woodstove to take the chill off the autumn evening. A comforting, welcoming warmth embraced him as soon as he walked through the door, and he could hear the fire snap and pop.

Something rich and spicy wafted from the kitchen, and his stomach growled. Must be that spaghetti sauce Joey had tried to get out of making, he thought.

Big band music was playing loudly on the stereo, and he could hear her singing along. Smiling, he followed the sound to the kitchen and leaned on the doorjamb to watch her bustle about. She looked breathtakingly vibrant and alive, with her luscious dark hair held away from her face with a bandanna rolled up for a scarf and her skin flushed from working.

It was a seductive thing to come home to, especially in the middle of a cold rain—a house that smelled like woodsmoke and other heady, delicious things, and a woman who managed to look both sexy and sweet while she was wearing an apron.

He must have made some sound because without turning around, she spoke. "Joey, I'm glad you're back. Would you mind running to the root cellar for more onions? This batch is not quite spicy enough for me."

He couldn't resist. "How spicy do you want it, Miz McPhee?"

She whirled around, nearly dropping her spoon. "Will! I didn't hear you come in. Where's Joey?"

"You plumb wore the boy out. I think he went home to get some sleep."

She looked puzzled. "He seemed fine a moment ago. Maybe he should think about quitting smoking if it makes him so tired."

He couldn't have stopped his laugh any more than he could have moved those mountains outside her window. "You know, darlin', I think he'll do exactly that, just as soon as this stakeout is over."

A grimace tightened her mouth. "This ridiculous stakeout should be over right now. You're just wasting everybody's time."

"I don't know. You seem to be getting a lot of work out of my boys."

She gave him a tart look. "If 'your boys' want to squander taxpayer's money hanging around here all the time, I'm going to see that at least somebody gets an honest day's work out of them."

"I think you're just trying to scare them all away," he said, tossing his Stetson onto the table.

"Is it working yet?"

"Not with me."

Andie watched as he edged away from the wall and advanced on her, his intent clearly visible in his eyes. She panicked.

"Will, you don't want to kiss me. Honest. I smell like onions."

"Mmm. I'm starving," he said, pursuing her like a hawk moving in on a helpless field mouse. "Besides . . ." He suddenly grinned. "I like it spicy."

She gave in to the inevitable and settled into his arms with a soft sigh. If she couldn't resist him when he was gruff and taciturn, how could she possibly fight him when he was teasing and laughing?

He was still cold from outside, and she rubbed her mouth against his to warm him.

"Mmmm. You can do that for about another four hours."

"Yeah, but then my spaghetti sauce will burn," she whispered.

"So will I," he whispered back.

He was already burning, she thought. She could feel the heat of him through the layers of cloth. Filled with a sudden, desperate need to be close to him—to savor every moment she had left with him—she tugged his heavy oiled coat off his shoulders and tossed it near his hat on the table, then tightened her arms around his neck and pulled him to her.

He groaned and deepened his kiss, pushing her back against the counter, as he had that night in his kitchen. His hands caressed the skin above the waistband of her jeans, and with each touch, she seemed to melt against him. It still wasn't close enough, she thought. She spread her legs so she could cradle his lean strength between her thighs, molding her body to his.

As always, she lost track of time while they kissed, while his thumbs danced over her skin, edging closer and closer to the undersides of her breasts beneath her shirt; while his mouth moved with tantalizing rhythm against hers; while those hot, glowing embers of desire he sparked so easily in her sizzled into a blistering, scorching need.

The phone and the timer on the stove rang at the same time.

Out of breath and flustered, Andie pulled away. She didn't know which to grab first, but Will moved to the stove in his long, easy stride and turned off the timer. Gone was the urgent, aroused lover of a few seconds before. Instead, he had that watchful, predatory look on his face, and she shivered as the phone rang again.

The strident call of the phone echoed through her

house, and reality came crashing back. She realized why he was standing there looking at the phone with an expression of anticipation on his face.

Her caller. How could she possibly have forgotten?

"Pick it up, Andie. Just try to act as natural as possible."

Heart still pounding from his kiss but her mouth suddenly dry with nerves, she crossed to it. She held a hand to her stomach in a futile effort to settle the nausea zinging through her.

"Come on, sweetheart. You can do this."

The phone rang again. She studied him for a moment, then took a deep, fortifying breath and picked up the receiver.

ELEVEN

"Hello," Andie said quietly.

Silence greeted her, and she felt her pulse kick up a notch. "Hello?" she repeated.

"Milagrita? Is that you?"

She practically sagged against the wall in relief as her mother's lilting voice traveled across the wires. "*Sí*, Mama."

"It did not sound like you at all," her mother said in Spanish. "Is something wrong?"

"No, Mama. Nothing's wrong." She crossed her fingers behind her back at the lie. Everything was wrong. She loved a stubborn wretch of a sheriff who would be riding into the sunset just as soon as he caught the bad guys.

She was living a damn cliché.

While she spoke with her mother, Andie watched Will out of the corner of her eye. He dipped a spoon into the batch of spaghetti sauce simmering on the stove and took a taste, closing his eyes in appreciation. He rinsed the spoon and drank some water, tilting his head back and exposing the skin below his chin, stubbled with the dark shadow of a day's growth. He opened her refrigerator and peeked inside in the eternal male quest for food.

These past five days of near-constant closeness with him had filled her with both joy and pain—joy that she would have these memories to comfort her when he left, and pain that she would have only the memories.

Although she'd tried to keep distance between them, tried to protect her heart, by the second day of the stakeout she realized it was an exercise in futility. The more time she spent with him, the more she grew to love him.

She loved the way he talked to the dogs every night when he came home. She loved the way he left his things around the house—his razor in the bathroom, his coat hanging on the peg beside the door. She loved the way he pulled her to him in his sleep, as if he couldn't bear to let her out of his arms.

She loved him.

Only half-listening to what Leticia said, she stayed on the line for several more minutes. Her mother must have sensed her distraction because she soon ended the conversation.

After she'd said good-bye and hung up the phone, Andie took a deep breath and turned back to Will. "My mother wants to come for Christmas."

"That will be nice."

Christmas. He'd be long gone by then, she thought, once again wrapped up in the vengeance that had come to consume his life. And she would be left trying to reglue the shattered pieces of her life.

She avoided his gaze and returned to the stove. "I need to get back to my sauce," she said, lifting the pressure cooker and removing it from the burner.

"Andie," he started, just as the phone rang again. Her mother must have forgotten something, she thought. Still with a hot pad in her hand, she reached for it.

"*Hola*, Mama," she said.

An ominous silence met her words, and she knew. She *knew* it was him. After a quick, panic-filled glance at Will, Andie drew a deep, calming breath.

"Yes? Hello?"

A dry raspy laugh rattled in her ear. "You're going to be begging for your mama before I'm done with you."

His eyes shuttered, Will picked up the cordless phone he'd made her bring down so whatever officer was on duty could listen in on the calls. Before pushing the Talk button, he stood behind her and whispered in her other ear, his breath barely a hushed outtake of air.

"Stay on the line. As long as you can, stay on the line so we can get a good trace. I know it's hard for you, but they're just words. Remember that, they're just words."

What a contrast, Andie thought, fighting an hysterical urge to laugh. The man she loved talking in one ear, the one she hated in the other.

She coughed to cover the soft intrusion of Will on the line as the caller continued what seemed like an endless succession of curses and threats. She knew she had to maintain the link, both so that the tracing equipment could work and so the tap they had on the phone would be supporting evidence in court. But it was hard. So hard.

She held out as long as she could, until her knuckles were clenched white, fighting every instinct in her that cried out to sever the connection. Just when she had reached the limit of her endurance, when she felt the panic clawing its way out, Will nodded to let her know enough time had elapsed for them to trace the call.

He gently took the phone from her and set it in its cradle as if it were made of fine porcelain. Then he pulled her into his arms and she collapsed against him.

"Easy, easy." He spoke to her slowly, with measured calm. "You did great, sweetheart."

"I'm such a baby, Will."

"No! You're not. You're the bravest woman I know."

She pressed her cheek to the cotton of his uniform, the hard, comforting muscles of his chest. She wanted to stay there forever, safe in the circle of his strong, capable arms. With a tenderness that brought a lump to her throat, he kissed her hair and tightened his arms for one more embrace, then reached behind her and dialed a number on the cordless phone. He'd explained the procedure to her before, and she knew he was calling the phone company to verify the location of the call.

"This is Tanner," he said into the phone. "Right. I need the last caller." Holding the phone in the crook of his neck, he whipped a pen out of his shirt pocket and scribbled a number on the memo pad by her phone. "Son of a bitch. Thanks."

He severed the connection and dialed another

number as Andie pulled away. Tension knotted in her stomach as she watched his face, its expression hard and intense. "Yeah," he said when someone answered on the other end, "Jessop's our guy. Round up Joe and Wade and have them meet me at the Rocking J."

She tried not to listen to the logistics of the arrest. She didn't want to know the details. She wanted to lock the door of the Limber Pine, to shut out the rest of the world and go back to the past five days where he'd been hers alone. When she'd been free to pretend, even for a little while, that this could go on forever.

Instead, she crossed to the stove and busied herself removing the jars from the pressure cooker.

After a couple more minutes of conversation, Will hung up the phone. "It's nearly over, Andie. A few more hours and Jessop will be behind bars."

She should be feeling some relief, shouldn't she? Instead, she had a terrible urge to cry. She shook it away and lifted another jar. "Now will you all leave me alone and let me get back to my life?"

"Even me?"

Especially you, she almost said. The lie clogged in her throat and nearly tumbled out. If she was smart, that's exactly what she should say. *Go away, Will. Go back to your desert and your real job and your grief.* She couldn't say it. Not with him watching her so closely, his eyes dark and piercing.

In the end, she didn't have to say anything.

"Never mind," he said, turning away and shrugging into his jacket. "Grab your coat. I'm taking you to the Bar W until we have Jessop in custody."

She laughed in disbelief and gazed at the bubbling

spaghetti sauce, the mess of her kitchen, the jars cooling on the counter. "I'm in the middle of something, in case it slipped your attention. I can't just leave."

"You'll have to. I'm sorry, Andie, but I can't leave you alone here. Not until he's in custody."

"Will—"

"I mean it, Andie. Anything could happen and I don't want to be so concerned for you that I can't concentrate during this arrest on the safety of my men."

A new, more intense panic whipped through her. Why had she never realized he could be in danger? That Tom might not take kindly to being arrested and might react violently?

She nodded and untied her apron.

A noise from the doorway distracted Andie from the magazine she was pretending to read. She looked up from her spot at the Bar W kitchen table to find Emily, wearing the oversized T-shirt she was using for pajamas, peeking her head around the doorjamb.

"What are you still doing up, Emily?"

The girl walked into the room and twisted her fingers together. "I couldn't sleep. Any word from my dad yet?"

"No, sweetheart. Not yet."

Emily shrugged and tried not to look concerned. "He'll call when he has a chance."

"You're probably right. Much more of this and I think I'm going to go look for him, though." Andie rose on the pretense of rinsing her coffee cup in the sink and glanced out the gingham-draped window, as she'd done at least a hundred times that night. Just as those ninety-nine other times, no headlights lit up the Bar W driveway. The drizzle had turned into a hard, cold Wyoming rain, the kind of night made for curling up in her favorite chair near the woodstove with a book and a mug of hot chocolate.

But there she was in a strange kitchen, drinking lukewarm coffee while perched on an uncomfortable wooden chair, and trying to convince herself the magazine article on beef production was the most gripping thing she'd ever read.

Andie would have laughed if she hadn't been so nervous over Will's safety.

Beth and Jace had tried to keep her company, but she'd forced them to go to sleep after she caught them each yawning for the fourth time. Dustin had colic, and she knew it was exhausting for both of them.

"I'll wake you when I hear something," she'd promised them, and for the last hour she'd kept a solitary vigil. It was nice to have company, she thought. Even the company of an eleven-year-old girl who didn't much like her.

She pivoted from the window and saw Emily settle into one of the chairs around the table and leaf through her magazine nonchalantly, though shadows of worry clouded those eyes that were so much like Will's.

"You'd better go on back to bed," Andie said. "You have school tomorrow."

"No, I don't. Parent-teacher conferences."

"Hmmm. In that case, I could use somebody to talk to," she admitted. "This waiting is terrible."

"You get used to it," Emily said philosophically.

"Sometimes in Phoenix he would have to be gone for a couple of days at a time. That was the worst. Mrs. Jenks—she's our housekeeper—would stay over and we had pizza and watched videos and it was pretty fun and everything. But I still missed my dad."

Andie fought a fierce longing to pull the girl into her arms, to put some laughter into those eyes that were too young to be filled with such sad wisdom. But she knew her sympathy would go over with Emily like a mouse at a cheese factory.

"Hey," she said instead, "Beth usually keeps some cookies stashed around here somewhere. Want to pig out with me while we wait for your dad to call?"

"She'll be mad if we eat 'em all."

"This is a crisis situation. She'll understand. You pour the milk and I'll see what I can scrounge up."

"Try the cupboard above the fridge." Emily flashed a wicked grin. "That's where I found 'em last time."

Andie clamped down on her lingering worry about Will, for the girl's sake if nothing else. She stood on tiptoe to reach into the high cupboard and emerged triumphant with an unopened bag of sandwich cookies.

"Bingo!"

Emily slid a glass of milk to her, and Andie ripped open the bag and placed some cookies on a plate. For a few minutes, they munched in companionable silence, broken only by the shifting and settling of the old house and the rain outside the window.

"So I have to ask you the question we all ask anybody under the age of eighteen. It's required," Andie finally said. "How's school going?"

"Okay." Emily twisted apart a cookie and scrapped the insides out before answering. "They're a ways behind what I was learning last year in Arizona so all the kids think I'm pretty smart. That's cool."

"You're in the sixth grade, right?"

Emily nodded. "Back home I'd be in middle school, but they keep sixth graders in the elementary school here. I feel like a baby with all those little kids."

"Is your class doing anything fun for the Halloween festival this year?"

"A spook alley. I get to dress up like a mummy and jump out from behind a coffin and scare people. It's way cool."

Andie gave a mock shudder. "I'm getting chills just thinking about it."

Emily grinned. "It won't be scary now. You'll know it's just me!"

Before she could answer, Dustin gave a soft cry from down the hall, and they both fell silent until his crying had stopped.

"He's a cute kid, isn't he?" Andie said, smiling.

"He's okay I guess. When he's not bawling."

She laughed. "It's hard when they have colic. But he'll grow out of it."

"The other day I was holding him and he was crying and I started tickling his tummy and he grinned. Just like that. Then he fell right to sleep. Aunt Beth says I have 'the magic touch.' Whatever the heck that means."

"It means you're good with kids. Not everybody is, you know, and it's a pretty special skill to have. You know," she continued, compelled to make the offer again, as she had the first day she met Emily, "I could use somebody with the magic touch at the school. Anytime you want to come and help, I'd be happy to have you."

Emily glanced down at the cookies, then quickly back up. "How about tomorrow? I don't have school and I don't have anything else to do except sit around here." She paused and looked away. "If you don't want me there, that's okay too."

Andie fought a powerful urge to reach across the space between them and hug the girl until her skittishness melted away. "Tomorrow would be great. I'll pick you up about eight. Think you can get up that early after this wild late-night girl party we're having?"

"Sure. I can if you can." Emily grinned and took another bite of a cookie.

Despite her nervousness over Will, a slow, comfortable satisfaction bubbled through Andie. She hadn't realized how much his daughter's antagonism bothered her until it was gone.

The phone hanging on the wall near the refrigerator suddenly rang, and they jumped.

Andie chuckled as they both scraped their chairs back to answer it. "Go ahead, Em. You take it." The girl dashed to the phone in a flurry of twirling T-shirt and skinny legs.

"Hi, Dad," she said after she'd answered it, her smile filled with exulted relief. No matter how rocky Will thought their relationship was, Andie mused, it was obvious Emily loved her father deeply.

"Yeah," Emily went on, "we were a little worried, I guess. Andie said if you didn't call soon she was going to come and look for you." She paused, then giggled. "I don't think she'd let me, but I could try."

She held her hand over the mouthpiece. "He said to grab you and lock you in the bathroom if you try to leave."

Andie smiled. For an instant while she listened to Emily's end of the conversation, she engaged in a wonderful, dangerous daydream. A daydream of happily ever after. A shimmering vision of the three of them forming a warm and loving family, filled with laughter and caring. It was so intense, so powerfully real, she could see it as vividly as she could see Beth's red-and-blue checked kitchen wallpaper.

But she knew, deep in her heart, that it could never be.

"Bye, Dad," Emily was saying. "Yeah, I know I need to go to bed. See you in the morning. I love you too." She turned and held the phone out to Andie. "He wants to talk to you."

Andie blinked away the images and took the phone, expecting Emily to go back to bed. Instead, the girl perched on a chair, her knees drawn up.

"Hi," she said softly into the phone. "You arrested Tom?"

"Yeah." She could hear the barely suppressed frustration in his voice. "For all the good it did us. He looked shocked as hell when we knocked on the door. Denies it all, of course. And now he's shut up tighter than a damn drum."

"Oh no, Will."

"He's got some hotshot lawyer flying in tonight from Cheyenne and refuses to answer any more questions until the guy gets here."

"Do you have to stay at the jail all night?"

He paused. "Hank says he'll take a guard shift."

The air in the kitchen seemed to drop twenty degrees, and Andie's hand felt clammy on the phone. She forced her breathing to steady.

"Hank's back?" she asked, staring blindly at the wall, at the checks that were merging into one big blur.

"Yeah. He heard what was going on and came down to see if he could help."

Already she could sense it, the distance he was putting between them, the clouds waiting just on the horizon to roll into her life and rip it apart. She had known all along he would leave. Why did it come as such a shock when the reality hit her?

"I'll probably be a few more hours," he added, "so why don't you just stay the night there?"

"No," she said immediately, driven by the need to return to her comfort zone. "I'd rather be home. I'll borrow a truck from here so I can sleep in my own bed. I have to check on the animals, anyway."

"Wait for me, then, and I'll pick you up after I'm done. I don't want you at the Limber Pine by yourself tonight."

She debated arguing with him, but she simply didn't have the energy. And deep in her heart, she admitted she wanted this night with him. Heaven only knew how many more she'd have, and she wanted to cling to him—to his strength and heat—as long as possible. Like the gray squirrels who lived in the big pine trees near her window, she wanted to store up these memories while she could. They would have to last her through all the bitter winters of the rest of her life.

She took a shaky breath. "All right. I'll wait for you. And, Will . . . I'm glad you're safe."

He paused, and when he spoke his voice was gruff. "I'm just glad it's over."

It's over. She closed her eyes. All of it. Soon he would be gone, and there was not one single thing she could do about it. She slowly hung up the phone and turned to look out the window over the sink. Her chest felt heavy and achy, her eyes scratchy, as if she had a cold.

It's over.

"You really care about my dad, don't you?"

In the midst of her upheaval, she had forgotten Emily. She wobbled for a moment, then forced a smile.

"Yeah, I do."

Emily looked down at the table. "You know, that night when I saw you guys kissing, it hurt. Right here." She rubbed the center of her chest. "I thought he was gonna forget my mom, just like I've started to forget her."

"Oh, Emily," she whispered.

"It's okay," the girl assured her solemnly. "I have some pictures of her, so I know I won't ever forget her. Not all the way. And you know what?" She flashed a grin. "I like my dad a lot better now, when he laughs again."

"He's a good man. And he loves you very much. Nothing will ever change that, sweetheart."

"I know." The girl looked down at the plate and fiddled with a cookie. "I'm—I'm sorry I was such a jerk the other day."

She loved the girl as much as she loved her father,

Andie suddenly realized. She pulled her into a quick hug. "Don't worry about it. Now you'd better scoot off to bed. It's hard work chasing after thirty preschoolers."

"Hard work?" Emily grinned again. "In that case maybe I better just stay here."

Andie smiled back. "You're not getting out of it that easily. I'll pick you up at eight."

She watched Emily walk down the hall, then tried to return to the magazine, knowing it was useless. All she could think about was Will and Emily and how empty her life would be when the two of them left.

The clock was just striking one when Andie heard an engine outside. She slid her chair back and hurried to the window as Will stepped out of one of the sheriff's department Broncos. A big vapor light illuminated the driveway, and she could see rain clinging to his brown hair. Even from this distance, he looked tired, with shadows under his eyes and the lines around his mouth scored deeper. He lifted his face to the rain and rotated his neck, then reached a hand to his shoulder and rubbed it through his jacket.

She hadn't even thought of his injuries in weeks, she realized. His shoulder must still be bothering him, but he didn't complain or even give any outward indication it so much as twinged.

Stubborn man. Stubborn, bullheaded, wonderful man. She blew out an exasperated breath that ended in a near sob as he headed up the walk. How would she ever get used to being without him?

"Hi," she said quietly, when he walked into the kitchen. She leaned against the sink and looked just past his shoulder, afraid he would read her thoughts in her eyes. The ten feet between them seemed huge, wider than the whole Whiskey Creek valley.

"Hi," he said. "I was hoping you'd have had the good sense to bed down here, instead of waiting up for me."

"Where'd you ever get the crazy idea I had good sense about anything?"

He walked a few steps closer. "You're right. What was I thinking?" A grin edged up the corners of his mouth.

She couldn't help the little laugh that sneaked out, but she quickly sobered. "I'm glad you're safe, Will," she said again. "I was so worried about you."

Their gazes locked and held, then he crossed the space between them and reached for her. She went willingly, gratefully, wrapping her arms around his waist, relishing the warmth of his body inside his jacket. He smelled like rain and cedar and pine, and she wanted to stay right there forever.

"Now you know how I've felt all damn week," he said gruffly. "Afraid to let you out of my sight, knowing Jessop was out there somewhere and there was not one single thing I could do about it."

"You did plenty, Will. You caught him, didn't you?"

"Yeah, we did." Male satisfaction resonated in his voice, and Andie smiled. He was still leaving and her heart was still breaking apart inside her. But for now they had this—their shared heat, their mingled heartbeats. It would have to be enough.

"Andie?" he whispered.

"Yes, Will?"

"It's late. Let's go home."

She closed her eyes, listening to his breathing, strong and steady, against her cheek.

Let's go home.

He could have offered her a trip to the moon, and it wouldn't have meant as much.

TWELVE

Like a phantom in the night, the dream crept over Will. Only when he was tangled in its sharp talons did he realize how long it had been since he'd been haunted by it.

He was no longer in Andie's big cozy bed, with her quilts tucked around him and her warm body in his arms. Instead, he was mowing his lawn in Phoenix, enjoying the ritual despite one-hundred-degree-plus heat that seared through his clothing, just as he'd been that Saturday afternoon when his life shattered.

The smell of exhaust mingling with the sweet, clean tang of fresh-cut grass reached him. He could feel the mower throbbing beneath his hands, hear its buzz, too loud because he needed to adjust the carburetor and he hadn't had much free time lately.

He'd been wrapped up in the biggest case he'd tackled yet, an intricate scheme of money laundering, racketeering, and drug-running over the border. He was close. He could feel it, taste it. Richie Zamora would be one hell of a collar. Maybe even get him a promotion. They could use the extra money with the baby on the way.

A flash of color on the porch caught his attention, and he turned to see Sarah smile and wave, holding a tray with a cold drink on it. She looked tired, he thought. The heat had been hard on her the past few weeks. She should have been lying down, especially since Emily was at a friend's birthday party for a few hours.

He waved back and turned off the mower, wiping the sweat from his forehead with the sleeve of his T-shirt. As he walked toward the porch, the sunlight glinted off her blond hair and the bright pink of her maternity shorts set, and he had the random thought that it was a classic suburban scene. *Ozzie and Harriet. Leave It to Beaver.*

Then suddenly it crumbled away, destroyed by raw violence.

Everything happened so quickly, as if somebody had punched the Fast-Forward button on a VCR. He felt the first bullet whiz past inches from him a millisecond before he heard its report, followed quickly by several more. Six. Seven. He didn't know. Years of instincts kicked in and he dived for the ground, reaching stupidly for his gun, as if he'd be wearing his shoulder holster with his cutoffs, and coming up with only empty air.

"Get down!" he yelled, and saw with relief that Sarah had ducked back into the doorway. In a split second, he judged the distance between him and the safety of the door and knew he wouldn't make it. His adrenaline pumping, he took the next-best option—the huge landscaping rock she'd insisted on, the one it had taken four of his buddies on the force to move into the yard. He inched toward it as the bullets continued to spit from the road.

Only then, when he was safely sheltered, did he think to look to the source of the bullets. Fury streaked through him. The glossy black Cadillac with its tinted windows and sleek chrome undoubtedly belonged to Zamora. With the windows down he had a clear view of the four bastards inside. He recognized every damn one of them, they hadn't even bothered to shield their identities.

He should have known Zamora would pull something like this. He should have known.

The scream of approaching squad cars reached them, and the men in the car fired off one last volley of shots before squealing off down the street. It didn't matter that they'd gone. He knew who they were and why they had come for him. And where to find them.

He scrambled to his feet as soon as they drove away. "They're gone, Sarah. You can come out," he yelled, racing toward the porch.

She didn't answer, but he didn't realize why until he reached the top stair and found her crumpled there on her side, an angry crimson stain soaking through the pink of her shirt. As it did every time he had the dream, his hoarse, anguished cry echoed in his ears, over and over. He rushed to her, never seeming to move fast enough, as if his feet were wedged in the cement of the steps.

He'd had the dream before. A thousand times. Always the same, the wild, choking panic, the terrible, consuming guilt. Knowing what he had to do, what he'd done a thousand times before. Will reached down to turn her, to gauge the extent of her injuries.

Only this time, when he turned her over, he jerked back, his breathing harsh and gasping.

Instead of Sarah with her gentle blond beauty, the woman lying motionless in front of him was Andie, with her little smile and her freckles and her dark, spiky lashes fanning cheeks as pale as the moon. It was her blood seeping onto the cream tile of his entryway, not Sarah's.

Will clawed his way out of the dream. He came back to reality in a rush of panic, to Andie's flowery bedroom, to her white cotton sheets that smelled of springtime. He could hear his blood pulsing in his ears and the soft sound of her breathing as he battled to return to consciousness.

He turned to reassure himself she was still lying there beside him, and he watched one corner of her mouth tilt up as she smiled in her sleep. As the thorny tendrils of the nightmare loosened their grip on him, as he watched her steady breathing, an even more terrifying thought swept through him.

He loved her.

The truth of it burned itself into his cells, seared into every inch of him. He loved her sweet generosity. Loved her caring, nurturing spirit. Loved her. She had thawed his heart and his soul, had replaced the grief with light and love, had taught him to laugh again.

He felt as if his whole life had been shaken, as if the earth had spun too far, too fast, had slid off its axis, and now everything was jumbled up. How could he have let it happen? Let a green-eyed sprite seep inside him, bringing her sunshine and her gentleness and her warmth.

With a sudden, savage longing, he wanted his grim life back. It was harsh and bleak, but it was safe, dammit. He didn't want this again, this vulnerability, this wild riot of feelings. He couldn't survive it.

He turned his head to her again and studied her features. The light outside her window had taken on the soft pearly hue of impending dawn, and she looked angelic lying there against the white of her sheets. So damn beautiful, with her long lashes and her full, generous mouth and that little mark just in the corner of her lips. He reached out to touch her hair, but curled his hand into a fist and let it fall to the pillow. He knew if he touched her, he would clutch her close and never let her go.

Andie awoke with a sour taste of foreboding in her mouth. Before she even opened her eyes, she knew he wasn't sleeping beside her. Funny how she'd gotten so attuned to him being there in the last week, how the rhythm of his breathing reached her, comforted her, even when she slept. And how his absence from her bed left such a vast, cold expanse.

She reached a hand out to the empty place beside her, then rolled onto her back. He was gone. Oh, probably not permanently yet, but it was only a matter of time.

The air in the room was chilled, she realized. Before too much longer, she was going to have to take a match to the pilot light in the furnace. But she knew no hot blast of forced air would melt the icy fear squeezing her heart.

She heard the door open and turned her head to find Will, dressed in a clean uniform, gazing at her through his shuttered gray wolf eyes. Something had changed. She knew it immediately, could see it in his face, feel it in the charged energy buzzing around the room. She didn't know what, exactly, but she could sense it.

Distance, she thought. He had put distance between them again. And even through the murky morning light, she felt his intense gaze, studying her features as if he were trying to memorize them.

"Good morning," she whispered, her voice hoarse with sleep and a weary resignation.

"I have to go."

By sheer force of willpower she stopped herself from flinching, from curling into herself. "I see."

"We're questioning Jessop again this morning. I should have been at the jail an hour ago."

She slid her feet out of bed and reached for her robe, struggling for some degree of normalcy. "I should be leaving soon too. Did I tell you Emily's coming to school with me this morning? I think she'll enjoy it. We're having Leaf Day today and going on a treasure hunt to see how many different kinds of leaves we can find." She was babbling and she knew he knew it.

"We need to talk, Andie."

Her gaze flew to his face. His features could have been carved from granite, they showed such little emotion.

"Now?"

The granite mask cracked a bit as a muscle flexed in his jaw. "No. Not now. But soon."

Soon. How she'd come to hate that word. Soon they would talk. Soon he would leave. Soon she would be alone again.

Emily was waiting for her when Andie reached the Bar W. She hadn't been sure whether to expect her or not, the events of the night before seemed so surreal now. Still, when she pulled into the long gravel driveway leading up to the ranch house, Emily was sitting on the front porch step in jeans and a sweatshirt, her hair pulled back in a ponytail.

As soon as Andie braked, Emily opened the door and climbed in, a wide grin on her face. "Cool. I finally get to ride in your truck."

Andie locked away the grim thoughts that had haunted her since Will had left her bedroom an hour earlier. "At last!" She summoned a smile. "Someone who appreciates a fine vehicle."

"I don't know about a fine vehicle. But I do like your truck!"

Emily spent the entire drive into Whiskey Creek admiring the floor gear shift, the broken speedometer with its big numbers, the huge padded seat that put them several feet off the ground.

When they arrived at Growing Minds, she hopped out with an eagerness that surprised Andie. She had to hurry after her, and Emily practically ran inside as soon as she'd unlocked the door.

Emily waited in the playroom while Andie hung up her jacket in her office. When Andie walked back out, she found Emily in the playhouse window, manipulating the mouse puppet on her hand.

"You're good at that," Andie told her.

Emily peeked her head up in the window, flushed, and pulled the puppet off her hand. "I was just playing around."

"If you want to, we could do a puppet show for the kids."

She shrugged. "Sure. Whatever."

"Let's wait until later, though, all right? The first thing I do in the morning is put out an activity for the children so they have something fun to occupy their interest as soon as they arrive. You probably don't remember being such a little kid, but some of them have a hard time watching mom and dad leave. Today I thought we'd paint first thing."

"What can I do to help?"

She gave the girl an approving smile. This Emily was a far cry from the sullen, uncommunicative girl she'd met a few months earlier. "I've got roll ends of newspaper print back in my office. They're pretty big, though. Do you think you can carry one?"

"Sure," she boasted. "I even helped Dad and Uncle Jace haul hay a few weeks ago."

"A measly little roll of paper is nothing to a girl who can lift a hay bale then."

Emily smiled back and walked into the office just as Andie heard the door to the center open. She turned, expecting one of her three assistants, but her welcoming smile faltered when she found a disheveled Marty Jessop looming in the doorway. He was wearing a long black oiled slicker, and she could hardly see his face in the shadow of his cowboy hat.

"Marty! Can I help you with something?"

The acrid smell of perspiration suddenly reached her, and as he looked at her, Andie took an instinctive step backward. His eyes burned in a too-pale face. "Is something wrong, Marty? Are you sick? Do you need me to call Doc Matthews?"

He speared her with his gaze, and she found she couldn't look away from the wild intensity blazing in his blue eyes. "You don't get it, do you?"

Andie felt behind her for the edge of the table, suddenly uneasy yet not knowing why. "Get what?"

"You shouldn't a had your stupid sheriff boyfriend arrest my dad. He didn't do nothin'."

Oh, dear. She'd been so relieved about Tom being in custody she hadn't given a thought to his son and what he must be going through, how hurt and embarrassed he would be.

"Look, Marty—"

"You shut up," he hissed. "Just shut up, schoolteacher."

Andie froze, her stomach roiling. *Schoolteacher.* The name her obscene caller always used for her. How could he possibly know that, unless—

She jerked her mind away from the idea. How could young Marty possibly be her caller? Yet as she stared at him, as she heard the echo of that low, disguised voice ringing through her mind, as she remembered the unsettling way Marty sometimes looked at her, the unthinkable didn't seem so far-fetched.

He must have seen the panic in her eyes, seen her realize the truth, because he reached inside his slicker and pulled out a sleek, sharp bowie knife, the kind used for skinning game.

She felt herself begin to hyperventilate and summoned every ounce of strength in her. She breathed slowly for precious seconds, her mind in a frenzy. Emily! She had to protect Emily, above everything else.

"Why don't you go on home, Marty?" she asked, striving desperately for calm. "I know you're upset about your father and you're not thinking clearly."

His harsh laugh sliced through the room. "My old man's going to give me up the first chance he has, to save his own damn hide. When your stupid sheriff finally figures it out, he's going to come lookin' for me."

Frantically, she looked around for some kind of weapon, but came up with nothing but soft cushions, toys, and art supplies, all chosen for their safety features. A preschool just wasn't the best place to come up with something handy to hurt somebody with, she realized. A hysterical giggle welled up in her throat, but she quickly swallowed it. Surely, if she concentrated hard enough, she could come up with some way to get both her and Emily out of there safely.

The whoosh of her office door opening interrupted her thoughts and her gaze flew to the hallway, where Emily walked out carrying the roll of paper. Marty was watching Andie, not the hallway, and she held her breath, praying he wouldn't turn around and see the girl.

Emily halted when she saw Marty, and she studied them for a few seconds, her gaze bouncing between the knife in Marty's hand and the wild panic on Andie's face. Then, very quietly, Will's daughter set down the roll of paper and eased back toward the rear door of the center.

As soon as she'd quietly opened the back door and slipped outside, Andie felt as if a weight the size of Wyoming had been lifted from her chest. She could figure out a way to get herself out of this, but it would be so much easier without having to worry about the girl's safety.

"Why don't you put that thing away?" she said to Marty. "You know you don't want to hurt anybody."

"It's all your fault, you know."

"My—my fault?"

"Yeah. I was just playing around on the phone. I never woulda hurt you." He reached out to touch her hair, and she fought to keep herself from flinching.

She held herself perfectly still, even when he yanked her hair, an ugly look on his face. "And then I saw you kissin' the sheriff and letting him touch you. You shouldn't a done that."

"I'm sorry," she whispered.

"You can tell me how sorry you are while we go for a little ride."

His fingers gouged into her arm as he yanked her toward the door. Andie's mind spun as she tried to think of some way to escape. He outweighed her by seventy-five pounds, most of that solid, farm-boy bulk. She could try outrunning him, but she hated to think what would happen if he caught her. Maybe it would be better to play along, to let him think she was cooperating until his guard was down.

She said the first thing that came to her. "Look, Marty. Let me . . . let me get my purse. Wherever we're going, we'll need money, won't we?"

He looked confused for an instant, but she didn't give him time to form an answer.

"I've got some," she said. "In my purse. And credit cards. I have those too. You can use them all."

He seemed to be considering it, then he nodded. "Okay. Good idea. We'll need gas. Just your purse, though, got it? That way everybody will think you just went out of town."

"It's—it's in my office."

She glanced at the clock. The other teachers would be arriving any moment now. She had to come up with something quick. What did she have in her office she could use as a weapon? Scissors? Nail file? What? *Think, Andie!* Suddenly it came to her. On her desk was a fossil paperweight the size and weight of a brick that Carly had given her for her birthday earlier that summer. If she could figure out a way to slip it into her purse, she could swing the whole thing at him, and if she aimed well and luck was on her side, she might be able to knock the knife out of his hand.

Her stomach twisted at the idea, but what other choice did she have? She would do anything to protect the children and the other teachers.

He watched her from the doorway as she grabbed her purse from underneath her desk. Blood rushing through her ears, she pretended to stumble as she rounded the desk and she reached for it, as if to steady herself. In the confusion, she grabbed the fossil and slipped it into her purse.

"Move it, schoolteacher. We're going to walk out real slow now. If anybody's watchin', they'll think we're just goin' for a little stroll. Got it?"

She tightened her grip on the purse. "Sure, Marty. Whatever you say."

Reflected light glinted off the sharp blade of the

knife as he gestured for her to leave first. Her knees shaking and her nerves screaming, Andie kept one eye on him and one on the knife, waiting for an opportunity to act. She pushed the door open and walked outside. Sunlight had replaced the clouds from the night before, but the air was still cool and smelled like pine. The door clicked shut behind him.

If she was going to do this, she would have to do it soon, Andie thought as she walked down the path. Like now. She took a deep breath, turned, and swung the purse with all her might. Propelled by the weight of the rock, it connected to flesh with a solid thunk. Marty grunted in pain and staggered back against the door. She'd missed his hand, but in his shock, he relaxed his grip on the knife and it flew from his hand, landing a few yards away.

She lunged for it, but before she could close her fist around it, pain exploded in the back of her head, the breath whooshed out of her, and she collapsed on the sidewalk.

His gun drawn, Will rounded the corner of the preschool at a dead run, just in time to see Andie grab for a knife on the ground and Jessop's bastard of a son drive the heel of his cowboy boot into her head.

He watched her crumple, her hand still outstretched. *No!* his mind screamed. He thought he said it out loud, but only the sound of Jessop muttering wild curses reached him.

Will started to move toward Andie, just as he realized she was breathing and conscious. The kick must have only dazed her. Relief flooded through him, and he offered up a quick prayer of thanks to a God he'd long since given up on, the one he'd been praying to ever since Emily ran into the jail a few minutes before, crying hysterically about how some bad man had Andie.

He hadn't taken time to do more than push Emily into Shirley's ample, comforting arms and shout orders for backup, then he had raced down the street, fury and a terrible, consuming fear churning in his gut.

Now, before he could react, before his lawman's instincts could kick in, he realized Jessop had grabbed the knife and scooped Andie to her feet. Damn. Why hadn't he moved faster, taken Jessop out while she was still down?

"Why'd you do that, schoolteacher?" Jessop said. "Why'd you hurt me?"

She shook her head groggily, as if to shake him off, but he only tightened his grip.

"Fight all you want, but you're not getting away from me. You hear me?"

"Drop it, Jessop!" Will yelled. "Let her go."

Marty turned to Will, panic flickering through his eyes. His hand flexed on the knife and he brought it to Andie's throat.

"Back off, Sheriff. Just let us walk outta here."

"You're not going anywhere. You know you don't want to hurt her. Just drop the knife and let her go."

Jessop gave a hysterical laugh that sent eerie tremors down Will's spine. "You don't think I can do it, do you? One good swipe, right here"—he pressed the wickedly sharp blade to her carotid artery—"and she'd bleed to death before you could reach her. You want that, Sheriff?"

Despite the chill of the October morning, a drop of sweat trickled down the back of Will's neck. He felt his nerves tighten, felt his shoulder cramp from holding his gun so steady.

Son of a bitch. Before his injury, he could easily have taken out a measly kid with a bowie knife, from twice the distance and in the middle of a damn dust storm if he'd had to.

He'd regained much of his strength, but he didn't know if he had the precision back yet.

"Look, Jessop. Don't make it worse for yourself. Drop it."

"I got nothing left to lose. I let her go and you're just going to arrest me anyway. You can't shoot me without shooting her too."

Jessop applied a subtle pressure to the blade. "Now leave us be, Sheriff, and I won't hurt her."

Will felt all the breath being squeezed from his lungs as a tiny dot of blood appeared in the pale skin of her neck. Andie's gaze met his, and he nearly staggered at the trust there.

Suddenly, the fear melted away, leaving only the rage pulsing through him, steady and strong.

She trusted him. Whether or not he was worthy of that faith didn't matter one damn bit. Andie was counting on him to keep her safe, and the assurance gleaming in her green eyes told him she had every reason to believe he would.

Sarah's face suddenly replaced Andie's. She'd trusted him, too, and he hadn't been able to protect her. If anything happened to Andie because he couldn't move fast enough, couldn't aim true, he might as well take his service revolver and point it at his own head.

He couldn't let her be hurt. He wouldn't. Not this time, dammit. He focused all his concentration on the Glock's grip, letting it become an extension of himself. He shut out the world, the deputies he knew were right behind him, the crowd that had gathered in the storefronts.

"Last chance, Jessop," he said, suddenly calm. "Drop it unless you want a bullet hole messing up that fancy coat of yours."

"You want to risk your girlfriend's pretty neck? Go right ahead and shoot me, then."

Will shrugged, squeezed the trigger, and watched Jessop go down, clutching his arm and leaving Andie standing alone as the knife fell harmlessly to the ground.

THIRTEEN

"How's the head, hon?"

"Feeling pretty stupid right about now," Andie told Carly, the latest in a long string of people calling to inquire about her health. She should have known word would travel faster than a runaway train in Whiskey Creek. A real live shootout on Main Street was about the most exciting thing to happen in town since Lizzie Kramer took too much cold medicine last fall and thought for a few hours she was Lady Godiva.

"You should be feeling incredibly lucky," Carly retorted. "If Emily hadn't been at the school to run for help, who knows what might have happened to you."

Andie cradled the cordless phone on her shoulder and reached up to clip a withered climbing rose off the lattice of her porch. The rain of the day before had swept out of the valley, leaving the air crisp and clean; and the trees, in all their vivid splendor, shone in the late-afternoon sun. Without any kind of cloud cover, it would be a cold one tonight, she thought irrelevantly.

"I would have come up with something sooner or later," she told Carly.

"Always the optimist, aren't you? Would you like me to come out to stay there tonight? Chase left this afternoon for San Francisco, and I think Jake can handle things on his own here at the ranch tonight. We could stay up all night and eat popcorn and talk about boys."

Andie summoned a laugh. "Another time, Carly. Okay?"

"Sure, sweetie. The offer stands."

"Thanks."

Carly hung up a few minutes later after receiving Andie's assurance that she wouldn't do anything too strenuous for the rest of the evening. It seemed a moot point after she'd just spent the day with thirty over-excited preschoolers. She'd forced herself to stay at Growing Minds, though her head had pounded as if a whole roomful of carpenters were working on it and her stomach had been twisted with nerves.

It had been pride at first, and then, when reaction set in, she'd decided she was better off working, keeping active.

Now she just wanted to disconnect her phone—the blasted thing that had started the whole trouble—and collapse.

She reached a hand to the back of her head and felt where Marty had kicked her. It had bled a little, and she had a bump the size of Kansas back there, but Doc Matthews had said there was no real damage.

Her head would be fine. Her heart? That was another story entirely. All because of one stubborn sheriff with aching eyes and a deadly aim.

After calmly shooting Marty Jessop in the shoulder—something folks in Whiskey Creek would be talking about for a long, long time—he'd checked to make sure she was safe, then handcuffed a hysterical Marty.

Doc Matthews had determined that the bullet merely grazed Marty—just enough to compel him to drop the knife. Marty was now in the Whiskey Creek jail, awaiting his preliminary hearing on assault and attempted kidnapping charges.

And Will? He'd been as remote and taciturn as he was when he first came to Whiskey Creek.

Andie sighed and settled onto the porch swing, pulling her sweater tight around her against the early evening chill. She shouldn't just sit there, she thought, not with all she had to do. The garden needed a layer of mulch for winter. The leaves needed to be raked. One more tree of apples needed to be harvested. But she could barely summon the energy to make the porch swing move.

No. She had responsibilities, she reminded herself. As much as she would have liked to spend one day—just one day—doing absolutely nothing, the ranch had to come first.

She was spreading grain for the chickens and watching them peck at the ground when his Jeep pulled into the driveway. Brushing her hands off, she straightened and watched him walk toward her.

Sunlight glinted off his hair, and his shoulders looked impossibly broad as he neared, and she wanted to run to him and bury herself against him. She didn't, though. The remoteness in his eyes stopped her.

"How's your head?" he asked.

She grimaced. "If one more person asks me that question today, I'm going to start wearing a sign. I'm fine, thank you."

"Doc Matthews said you'll have a bump, but nothing serious."

"When did you talk to him?"

"You think I would have let you keep working all day if I hadn't checked with him first?"

She fell silent as the image flashed through her mind of him calmly taking aim and squeezing the trigger. How had he been so cool about it when, nearly eight hours later, she still didn't feel as if her heart had slowed?

"I didn't have a chance to say thank you, Will. For riding to my rescue the way you did. Just like Marshal Dillon." She tried to smile, but couldn't seem to work the right muscles. Not with him standing there so distant. "You're a pretty good shot, Sheriff."

He looked out at the mountain, then back at her. "I'm not the sheriff anymore," he said quietly.

She'd known. Somehow she'd known.

"Hank's back on the job. I quit an hour ago."

"So when do you leave?"

"Andie—"

"When do you leave, Will?" she interrupted him. "You might as well get it over with and tell me."

"Now. Tonight."

Her hands started to shake, so she shoved them into the pockets of her sweater, encountering a few hard kernels of grain that must have fallen there. She pinched them between her thumb and forefinger as she tried to regain control.

"I see," she said, with what she hoped was calm acceptance in her voice.

"I had a phone call from Phoenix this afternoon. My captain called to tell me I'm not on probation anymore and to tell me, strictly off the record, that he had a good solid tip where Zamora might be hiding. I need to follow it up, Andie. I have no choice."

"That's the only reason you're leaving, then? This call from your captain?"

"I would have left anyway," he admitted. He leaned against the split-rail fence. "With Hank back on the job and Marty in custody, there's nothing left for me to do in Whiskey Creek."

Except stay right here and love me, she thought. She bit her lip to keep it from trembling, to keep the words from spilling out. "Do you . . . do you need any help packing?"

"No. I'll send for the rest of my things in a few weeks, if that's all right. Beth says she'll take care of everything."

"What about Emily?"

"We talked it over and decided she would stay with Beth until the school semester is over at Christmas time. It's better this way."

"Better for whom?" Anger began to seep through the cracks in her heart, and she clenched her fists in the pockets of her sweater.

"For everybody. For Emily. For me. For you. I have to go, Andie. Can't you see that?"

"No," she snapped, hating herself for her bitter tone but unable to temper it. How could he walk away from what they had together? "I don't see it at all."

"You were almost killed today. Do you have any

idea what the thought of that does to me, what I went through when I saw you go down?" The gray of his eyes darkened nearly to black. "It rips me apart. I saw you lying there and it was just like before. Like Sarah."

It was the first time she'd ever heard him say his wife's name. For some reason, that knowledge—that he'd so carefully kept this part of himself away from her—hurt far worse than knowing he was leaving.

"I couldn't protect her, Andie. I should have been able to, should have known Zamora was serious when he threatened me. Because I screwed up, my wife and son died. When I saw Jessop with that knife to your throat, it was the same damn thing. I should have known. Something didn't feel right about the whole thing, about arresting Tom. But I didn't listen to my own instincts, and as a result you could have died."

"I didn't, though, Will. I'm fine."

"No thanks to me."

"What do you mean, no thanks to you? You're the one who ended up shooting him."

"Which was one hell of a stupid thing to do when you were standing right next to him. I didn't even think about it, didn't think about what would have happened if I'd missed. Don't you get it, Andie? It never should have happened. I should have been able to protect you. Just like I should have been able to protect Sarah and I couldn't."

"I don't need you to protect me, Will. Just to love me."

The words slipped out and she would have given anything to call them back. His jaw clenched and he reached a hand toward her, then dropped it.

"I can't. Dammit, Andie, I can't."

"Who are you trying to convince? Me or yourself?"

"Andie—"

"It doesn't matter," she said, hugging her arms around herself. "It doesn't. Just—just be safe, Will. Please?"

He turned and walked a few paces, then looked back. He studied her out of eyes that were once again as bleak as a winter sky. A hawk spiraled overhead, piercing the air with its eerie, mournful cry, and the wind moaned in the pine trees. The sounds echoed the pain pulsing through her. But she wouldn't beg. Dammit, she wouldn't beg.

Despite her strenuous efforts to keep it in check, one stubborn tear slipped from her eye. She could feel it rolling down her cheek. If anything, Will grew more stoic, and then, with a strangled groan, he crossed the space between them and swept her into his arms, crushing her so tightly, the buttons of his shirt pressed into her skin through the layers of cloth. He lowered his mouth to hers, and she tasted desperation and regret in his kiss.

"I'm sorry, Andie," he whispered against her lips. Then he turned and walked away, leaving her standing there, one arm tucked against her stomach, the other hand pressed to her mouth.

As he drove out onto the road, the wind sent a torrent of leaves rattling behind him.

"Well, guys," Andie said, "it looks like our gardening days are over for the year."

The dogs barked and raced off to chase one of the chickens that had ventured from the pen to bravely peck the cold, hard ground. The weak early morning sun filtered through the trees, sparkling off the frost that coated every surface.

Her breathing made little puffs of condensation in the cold air as Andie studied the blackened remnants of her garden, all that remained of it, anyway, the few plants the frost hadn't destroyed.

She felt just like her frost-killed garden, as if all the life had been frozen out of her. To her shame, she'd spent the night alternating between grief and anger, had lain in her bed, under her wedding-ring quilt, crying more tears than she ever thought she contained.

And where had it gotten her? Exhausted and wrung out, with nothing left in her but a weary acceptance. Around about dawn, she'd come to the realization that no matter how hard she cried, Will was still gone and there was not one single thing she could do about it except try to rebuild her life once again.

She ought to be pretty darn good at that, she thought, grimacing. She'd certainly had enough practice.

Sighing again, she made her way across the ground, the frost crunching beneath her boots, to her garden bench. She would go on. With hard work and practice, she might even achieve some measure of peace again.

The preschool didn't open for another hour. That should give her just enough time to make a start on that apple tree, she decided.

She was up on the ladder, filling her second bucket, when she heard a vehicle pull into the driveway. Beth must be checking up on her, she thought. She hoped the cold had wiped away all traces of her self-pity. It wouldn't do for Will's sister to know how much his leaving had devastated her.

She picked a few more apples, then started to climb down, just as a deep, dearly familiar voice vibrated through the cold air.

"You missed a few up there."

Her heart stumbled for an instant and she froze. She followed the voice and found him standing at the bottom of the ladder, watching her with a curious, tender expression on his face.

"I—I think you took a wrong turn somewhere, Sheriff," she said breathlessly. "Phoenix is a few miles south of here."

"You know, I was halfway through Utah before it hit me."

"What hit you?"

"Come down and maybe I'll tell you."

Her hands shaking, she slid the rest of the way down the ladder and faced him, her blood throbbing rapidly through her, her chest tight.

"About two in the morning," he said, "I drove through that empty stretch in Utah. You know, where the mountains begin to turn into desert. As I looked out at all that sagebrush, I suddenly realized there's nothing for me in Phoenix. Just dust and heat and one hell of an empty life. Everything important to me is right here."

Her heart quickened a pace but she refused to let herself hope. Not yet.

"Emily?" she asked.

He stepped closer to the ladder, caging her between it and his body. Strong fingers caressed her cheek and his wolf eyes burned with intensity.

"Yeah, Emily. And somebody else."

She swallowed down the beginnings of a smile. "Beth?"

He gave a raspy laugh. "You're not going to make this easy on me, are you?"

"After what you put me through last night? What do you think?"

He framed her face in his big, hard, wonderful hands. "All Phoenix can offer me is vengeance and hate. If I went back, if I followed that trail, it would eventually destroy me. Wyoming, on the other hand, has the one thing I can never give up. You."

Her smile broke free just as he dipped his head and whispered his lips against hers. Her hands fluttered up and rested against his chest, and she settled into his kiss.

All the pain of the night before seemed to shimmer away as she felt his muscles, his strength, beneath her fingers.

"I love you, Andie. I think I have since the moment I pulled you over that day, when you flashed that smile and your long legs and offered me a drink."

She laughed against his mouth and wondered if she'd ever get used to hearing those words.

"And here I thought you meant all that frowning and growling you did," she teased.

"I thought I did too." He paused, staring into her eyes. "I never thought I'd love another woman after Sarah died. Never deserve to love another woman."

"Oh, Will. You're not to blame for your wife's death. You're not!"

"A part of me will always feel guilty for it, Andie, will always wonder what I could have done differently. But the rest of me is just thanking God I have another chance for love."

"I do love you," she whispered. "So much, Will."

He cleared his throat. "I don't know how we'll get along, but I thought I'd see if Hank could use another deputy around here. If he doesn't, maybe I could try my hand at ranching again. If you're willing to marry a broken-down ex-sheriff, I'm even willing to put up with that mangy goat of yours."

She started to laugh, then the rest of his words sank deep into her bones and she gaped at him.

Marry him? *Marry* him? She couldn't possibly. She didn't dare. Slowly, she pulled her hands from around his neck and slid from the ladder, away from him.

"I . . . Can't we go on as we have been?" she asked, knowing even as she said it that it was impossible. For Emily's sake, if nothing else.

He looked confused. "I want to marry you, Andie. To live here at the ranch, if that's what you want, and to see those mountains out the window while I kiss you awake every morning for the rest of our lives."

She wanted that too. Desperately. The pain of the night before paled compared to this agony, the terrible knowledge that he loved her as she loved him, but that she could never be with him.

"I can't marry you, Will."

"What do you mean, you can't marry me? I love you. You just said you love me. Isn't marriage the normal progression of things, or have I missed a step somewhere?"

"No. I just . . . I should have told you before now."

"Told me what?"

She wrapped her arms around herself as Peter's words echoed in her ears. *I don't want you now. I can't.*

"Marriage is about family. Children. I—I can never give you that."

What the hell was she talking about? Will wondered. He started to speak, but her outstretched hand stopped him.

"I told you about the baby and the miscarriages," she continued in that dry, lifeless tone he'd heard only once before. "I . . . What I didn't tell you is that the last baby was too much for me and I—I had to have an emergency hysterectomy. I can't have children."

Stunned, he could do nothing but stare. It explained so much about her, he realized. The caring she dispensed to everyone around her. The ranch that flourished under her loving attention. The school, where she spent each day taking care of other people's children.

She was doing her damnedest to make up for the loss of something that had been so important to her, and it nearly broke his heart. Just when he thought he couldn't love her any more, she managed to spin him around once again.

"Oh, Andie. You're what I want. You. The sweet, funny, generous woman who thawed my heart. I don't need a brood mare. I need you."

"What if you decide in a year or two that you want a child?"

"I have a child, Andie. And so will you, if you marry me. A beautiful, stubborn daughter."

Tears filled her eyes, shimmering in the deep green. "How can you take that risk? What if you decide you want another child, and that I'm not good enough anymore because I can't give you that?"

Not good enough? Where the hell was this coming from? He suddenly remembered her talking about her marriage, about her husband who had desperately wanted a child. About his wealthy parents and their constant demands. Was that the reason she was divorced? Because her husband couldn't deal with the fact that she could no longer give him what he wanted?

Something of his fury must have shown on his face, because she seemed to shrink inside herself.

"I'm so sorry, Will. I should have told you before."

Though the rage still thrummed through him at the spineless bastard she'd married, Will struggled to contain it and to choose just the right words that would convince her it didn't matter to him.

"Andie. I love you," he said slowly. "No matter what. You healed me, sweetheart. Taught me to laugh and to love and to live again."

She closed her eyes, as if his words hurt her somehow, and he knew he had to try harder. "Andie, whatever happened to you is not your fault. Just like what you said about me not being to blame for Sarah's death. It doesn't make you any less of a person. If anything, it only makes me love you more because you've worked so hard to make your life right again."

Andie lifted her head, afraid to hope. The possibility of a future with Will and Emily was like a shimmering mirage, just out of reach.

"I'm sorry for what happened to you," he continued. "So sorry. And I want to spend the rest of my life trying to make it not hurt you so much." He reached for her hand with both of his and held it tightly. "I can't guarantee I'll succeed, but I'll do my damnedest."

"Oh, Will," she whispered. She felt a smile bubbling up inside her at this earnest, tender side of him, which she'd never imagined lurked inside her gruff sheriff.

He tugged her closer to him. "I swear to you here and now that you and Emily will always be more than enough family for me. And that I will wake up every single day for the rest of my life thanking whatever miracle brought me to you."

"Oh, Will," she whispered again, awed by the sweetness of it, by the promise shining in his silver eyes, by the calm assurance sweeping away every single one of her doubts like a healing breeze after the storm. "Are you sure?"

"As sure as those mountains, Andie," he said solemnly, sincerely, and she fell into his arms.

He held her tightly, nearly squeezing the breath out of her. "Is that a yes?"

Her smile broke free just as the last of the frost melted in the sunlight. "That's a definite yes, Sheriff."

EPILOGUE

He was about to break a promise and the knowledge terrified him.

Nervousness edging through him, Will quietly opened the door to the ranch house. The house smelled alluringly of gingerbread and cinnamon mixed with the sweet tang of pine from the huge Christmas tree in the front room and the evergreen garlands Andie and Em had draped around the house.

He crunched the snow off his boots and hung his Stetson on the rack beside the front door before poking his head into the living room, where Bing Crosby sang about chestnuts and open fires at an ear-splitting level and the lights on the tree shimmered and winked.

The dogs, lying on their favorite rug near the woodstove, thumped their tails in greeting, but didn't rise to greet him.

Familiarity breeds contempt, Will thought, chuckling. A year ago, they would have been all over him, barking a frenzied greeting. Now he only merited a measly tail wag.

His life had changed completely in the past year, he thought. He took off his coat, the one with the sheriff's star proudly displayed, and hung it on the rack.

There was another way it had changed, and he hadn't even had to resort to ranching. He'd returned from his honeymoon with Andie to find two messages on the answering machine at her ranch. One had been from his old boss in Phoenix telling him Zamora had been captured the day of Will's wedding and would spend the rest of his life in prison. The other had been from Hank, saying he was quitting for good and that the town wanted Will to take over.

He'd found more contentment than he ever thought possible in Whiskey Creek. A job he'd grown to love. A daughter who had once again become sweet and affectionate. And most of all, Andie.

He found her in the kitchen, wearing an apron covered in flour-frosted poinsettias over a fancy velvety green dress that perfectly matched her eyes. Her hair was piled on her head, and long diamond earrings swayed when she moved.

All dressed up and she still couldn't stop working, he thought with a grin. She was singing loudly and off-key with Bing about kids from one to ninety-two, and he wondered if he could possibly love her any more.

He walked up behind her and pressed his lips to the nape of her neck, just under her upswept hair, and she jumped, nearly spilling the bowl of dough on the floor.

She whirled around. "Will! I hate it when you scare me like that. Next time make some noise when you come in!" Despite her scolding tone, her eyes lit up and her mouth softened with welcome.

"Next time turn down the stereo. You couldn't hear a damn stampede in here."

"I like my music loud," she retorted.

"Yeah, sweetheart, I think everybody in the county has realized that by now."

She gave him a mock frown that was so adorable he just had to try to kiss it away. Before his lips met hers, he paused. "You have flour on your cheek, Mrs. Tanner."

"Rats." She backed away from him and rubbed her face. "And I was trying so hard to stay clean."

He leaned back against the counter. "Don't you think you might be a tad overdressed for making cookies?"

She frowned again. "I started worrying I might not have baked enough, so I thought I'd whip up one more batch while we waited for you. You're late, by the way."

"I ran into a little delay." Knowing he was stalling, putting off the inevitable while he tried to form exactly the right words, he reached around her for one of the sugar cookies cooling on the rack. She swatted his hand before he could grab one.

"Stop that," she ordered. "Those are for your sister's party. Speaking of which, you need to hurry and shower if we're going to make it on time."

"Beth'll keep. I'm very much afraid this won't." He pulled her against him and lowered his mouth to hers.

A year of marriage, and just being close to her still made his head spin. He knew, with male arrogance, that he had the same effect on her because she melted in his arms, oblivious to the snow falling outside, to the party starting in less than an hour, to the timer buzzing on the stove.

He swallowed her low moan just as he heard the sound of a throat being cleared loudly.

He glanced over to find Emily standing in the doorway. "If you two are quite finished"—Em had on her exasperated prissy tone again, he noticed with amusement—"I have two more presents to wrap and I am out of tape. Where could I find some more?"

Andie, flustered, pulled out of his arms and turned off the timer, then rummaged through a drawer near the refrigerator. She handed a roll to Emily. "Here you go, sweetheart. Do you need help?"

"No. I'm just about through. Besides, it's your present I'm wrapping."

"Then you ought to need lots of tape. It's big, right?" Andie asked, a hopeful note in her voice, and Emily shook her head.

"You're as bad as Aunt Beth. You'll just have to wait until tomorrow."

"I'm not the one who's been rattling every present under the tree for weeks now, young lady."

Emily just grinned at her. "I know. That was Dad!"

They both laughed, and he took their ribbing with good-natured aplomb. He was used to it, after all, to them ganging up on him.

"Merry Christmas, Em," he said.

She smiled again and gave him a quick hug. "Merry Christmas, Daddy."

After she'd returned upstairs, he knew the time had come. He couldn't put it off any longer.

"Andie, we need to talk."

"Now? Will, we're going to be late." She continued moving cookies from the tray to a rack. "Go shower. We can talk after the party."

"I think you'll want to hear this."

Something in his tone must have alerted her he was serious, because she dropped the spatula, her face worried, and slid into a chair.

"What is it? What's wrong?"

He wished he knew what her reaction was going to be to what he had to say. It would make it so much easier.

"I had a call from a social worker this afternoon. Do you remember that car accident I was called out on last week near Pinedale, where that young couple was killed?"

She nodded, still looking confused.

"Seems they had two little kids who weren't hurt. A girl, Rosa, who's three and a baby boy, Antonio, just four months."

"Oh, the poor dears!" Her green eyes were drenched with compassion. "And right before Christmas. How terrible."

"That's what I said to this Mrs. Carlisle. The social worker. I guess they don't have any other family, and now she's looking for somewhere these two little kids can spend Christmas. Problem is, the girl doesn't speak English. Just Spanish. I guess Mrs. Carlisle knew about you and the preschool, knew you speak Spanish and that you're good with kids. She called me to see if these two little ones could stay here with us."

Andie immediately rose. "Of course! I wonder if we could get Walt to open the store for us so we could pick up a few presents for her to unwrap tomorrow. The girl can sleep in with Emily and I'm sure we can borrow that portable crib from Beth for the baby since Dusty's too big for it anymore."

She continued making plans, until he held out a hand.

"Andie. There's more."

"More?" She slid back into the chair.

"Mrs. Carlisle says they're looking to place the children with a family who might be interested in a more permanent situation."

"A—a permanent situation?"

"Adoption."

She stared at him as if he'd just yanked the chair right out from under her. He crossed to her and knelt so he could look into her eyes. "Look, I know when you agreed to marry me, I promised you that you and Emily would be enough family for me. And you are. I'll understand if you say no. I swear I will, sweetheart."

"Adoption . . ."

"It's just that these kids are all alone, Andie. They have nothing now and we have so much."

"Will—"

"I know, it's not fair for me to spring this on you when we haven't even talked about it." The thing was, he'd already fallen head over heels in love with the two the minute the social worker brought them into his office, Rosa with her shy smile and Antonio—Tony—with his big dark eyes and gurgling laugh.

"And Emily," he continued. "We should talk it

over with Emily. How would she feel about getting an instant brother and sister?"

"She'd think it would be pretty cool as long as she doesn't have to share her room," Emily said from the doorway. "And as long as she doesn't have to baby-sit all the time."

As if in a daze, Andie shook her head. A tendril of hair escaped to fall to her face. "Where are they?"

He straightened and felt himself flush. "Outside. I told Mrs. Carlisle to meet me here. She's waiting out there with them in her car. I would have called you, but I wanted to talk to you face-to-face about it. I was pretty sure you'd say yes, about Christmas, anyway. The rest of it, I told her we'd play by ear. I . . . I'll go get them."

When he returned to the kitchen, with Rosa holding his hand tightly, Andie was sitting in the same chair, still looking shell-shocked. Mrs. Carlisle walked in behind him, holding the baby.

The little girl watched out of huge solemn eyes, clinging to Will, as Andie stood and crossed to her.

"*Hola, querida,*" she said softly, holding out a cookie. The girl took it, then buried her face in Will's jeans.

"She's a little shy," Mrs. Carlisle said. "But she's a real sweetheart. So's this one." She held out the blanket-wrapped infant to Andie, who took him with a look of reverence on her face.

She peeled the blankets away and stared at the round cheeks, at the dark eyes watching with an unblinking stare, at the thick dark hair that dipped into the little boy's plump face.

Will watched a tear drip onto the baby's face, and

he suddenly felt unsure of himself. He'd hoped she would be happy about this. He knew she still yearned for a child, though she tried to hide it from him.

Had he only succeeded in bringing her more pain?

"Sweetheart, I'm sorry," he said, unable to bear it. "We can find somewhere else for them to spend Christmas."

"No, you will not," she said fiercely, hugging the children to her. "They're staying right here."

Mrs. Carlisle cleared her throat. "There are bottles and formula there for Antonio and enough diapers to get you through a couple of days at least. I'll check with you tomorrow to see how things are going. Now if you'll excuse me, my family's waiting for me."

Will hefted Rosa into his arms and walked back to the living room to open the door for the social worker. When he returned, Emily and Andie were both gazing down at the little boy.

As he watched them smile at the baby's gurgling and cooing, he had to fight down the ache in his throat at the incredible gifts he'd been given.

Emily. The verdant little ranch. The two sweet dark-eyed children who'd already sneaked into his heart.

And most of all, the beautiful, wonderful woman who'd made it all happen, who had healed him, who had coaxed him out of his ugly world of grief and vengeance, into one overflowing with life, with joy.

Andrea Milagros Tanner.

His miracle.

THE EDITORS' CORNER

May Day! Cinco de Mayo! Mother's Day! Memorial Day! Armed Forces Day! Okay, okay, that last one's a stretch, but hey, the merry month of May is a time to celebrate. May signals the beginning of summer, National Barbecue Month, picnics, fairs, and don't forget, four excellent LOVESWEPTs knocking on the door. This month's quartet of love includes a stolen dog, a sleepwalker, a man with a smile that should be registered as a lethal weapon, and a woman who picks herbs in the nude! How's that for reading variety?

Take one U.S. marshal, a feisty P.I., an escaped convict, and a stolen poodle, and you've got a surefire way of learning the **TRICKS OF THE TRADE**, LOVESWEPT #834 by Cheryln Biggs. Mick Gentry and B.J. Poydras have no reason to know each other—after all, he's from Nevada and she's from

Louisiana. But the two are destined to meet when his case takes a nosedive straight into hers. The spunky detective prefers working alone, which is just fine with the rugged marshal, but when clues keep leading them to each other, can he convince her to put aside their differences long enough to give love a chance? Cheryln Biggs ignites a sizzling partnership that's hotter than a sultry summer night in the Big Easy!

When Duncan Glendower watches Andrea Lauderdale sleepwalk straight into his bed and into his arms, he realizes that he's a goner in Kathy Lynn Emerson's **SLEEPWALKING BEAUTY**, LOVE-SWEPT #835. Haunted by events that refuse to let her sleep in peace, Andrea reaches out to him in the darkness, tempting him to break all his rules. Struggling to protect the troubled beauty in a remote lodge, Duncan knows that sharing close quarters with the woman he's always loved is risky at best. But can he help Andrea fight the fears that rule her and prove to her that he'll never let her go? Kathy Lynn Emerson explores a man's desire to protect what's precious in this deeply moving novel of passion and possession.

Worried that the deadly threats against her small airport are somehow linked to the arrival of charter pilot Dillon Kinley, Sami Reed must decide if she dares to trust a sexy stranger who is **CHARMED AND DANGEROUS**, LOVESWEPT #836, by Jill Shalvis. Flashing a killer smile and harboring a score to settle, Dillon informs Sami that he won't be an easy tenant to please. But when fury turns to tenderness and old sorrows to new longings, can Sami win her rebel's love? New to LOVESWEPT, Jill Shalvis beguiles readers with a breathless tale of revenge and remembrance about the rogue whose caresses make his cool-eyed spitfire shameless.

In **MIDNIGHT REMEDY**, LOVESWEPT #837, Eve Gaddy brings together a lady with a slightly sinful past and a doctor who's traveled miles of bumpy road to reach her. Piper Stevenson has supposedly cured one of Dr. Eric Chambers's patients with a mystical remedy that she refuses to share. When Eric lights a fire in Piper's heart, will this nursery owner allow herself to come out of the darkness and into the lightness of love? Eve Gaddy reveals a delectably funny and yet touchingly poignant romance that renews faith in the heart and tells of a forgiveness strong enough to last forever.

Pssst! Not to spoil a surprise, but . . . keep an eye out for some changes on the LOVESWEPT horizon when we bring back a new, yet traditional look to our covers!

Happy reading!

With warmest wishes,

Shauna Summers

Joy Abella

Shauna Summers

Joy Abella

Editor

Administrative Editor

P.S. Look for these Bantam women's fiction titles coming in May. New in paperback, **MISCHIEF**, from *New York Times* bestselling author Amanda Quick. Imogen Waterstone has always prided herself on being an independent young woman. Now she needs the help of Matthias Marshall, earl of Colchester, a man of implacable will and nerves of iron. But when the earl arrives, so does a malevolent threat that emerges from London, a threat sinister enough to endanger both their lives. And bestselling author Karyn Monk returns with **ONCE A WARRIOR**, a passionate medieval tale that sweeps you away to a remote fortress in the Scottish Highlands, and the man who must fight to win the heart of his beautiful princess. Ariella MacKendrick needs a hero and she has only a seer's visions to guide her to the Black Wolf, a knight of legendary strength and honor with a vast army. A fire still rages in his warrior heart, but can love transform him into a hero? And immediately following this page, preview the Bantam women's fiction titles on sale *now*!

For current information on Bantam's women's fiction, visit our new Web site, ISN'T IT ROMANTIC, at the following address: **http://www.bdd.com/romance.**

Don't miss these extraordinary
women's fiction titles by your
favorite Bantam authors

On sale in March:

A THIN DARK LINE
by *Tami Hoag*

THE BRIDE'S BODYGUARD
by *Elizabeth Thornton*

PLACES BY THE SEA
by *Jean Stone*

*When a sadistic act of violence
leaves a woman dead . . .
When a tainted piece of evidence
lets her killer walk . . .
How far would you go to see justive done?*

A THIN DARK LINE

the new hardcover thriller
by *New York Times* bestselling author

Tami Hoag

*When murder erupts in a small Southern town, Tami
Hoag leads readers on a frightening journey to the shadowy
boundary between attraction and obsession, law and justice—and exposes the rage that lures people over a thin
dark line.*

*Her body lay on the floor. Her slender arms outflung,
palms up. Death. Cold and brutal, strangely intimate.*

The people rose in unison as the judge emerged
from his chambers. The Honorable Franklin
Monahan. The figurehead of justice. The decision
would be his.

*Black pools of blood in the silver moonlight. Her life
drained from her to puddle on the hard cypress floor.*

Richard Kudrow, the defense attorney. Thin,
gray, and stoop-shouldered, as if the fervor for justice
had burned away all excess within him and had begun
to consume muscle mass. Sharp eyes and the strength
of his voice belied the image of frailty.

Her naked body inscribed with the point of a knife. A work of violent art.

Smith Pritchett, the district attorney. Sturdy and aristocratic. The gold of his cufflinks catching the light as he raised his hands in supplication.

Cries for mercy smothered by the cold shadow of death.

Chaos and outrage rolled through the crowd in a wave of sound as Monahan pronounced his ruling. The small amethyst ring had not been listed on the search warrant of the defendant's home and was, therefore, beyond the scope of the warrant and not legally subject to seizure.

Pamela Bichon, thirty-seven, separated, mother of a nine-year-old girl. Brutally murdered. Eviscerated. Her naked body found in a vacant house on Pony Bayou, spikes driven through the palms of her hands into the wood floor; her sightless eyes staring up at nothing through the slits of a feather Mardi Gras mask.

Case dismissed.

The crowd spilled from the Partout Parish courthouse, past the thick Doric columns and down the broad steps, a buzzing swarm of humanity centering on the key figures of the drama that had played out in Judge Monahan's courtroom.

Smith Pritchett focused his narrow gaze on the dark blue Lincoln that awaited him at the curb and snapped off a staccato line of "no comments" to the frenzied press. Richard Kudrow, however, stopped his descent dead center on the steps.

Trouble was the word that came immediately to Annie Broussard as the press began to ring themselves around the defense attorney and his client. Like every other deputy in the sheriff's office, she had hoped against hope that Kudrow would fail in his attempt to get the ring thrown out as evidence. They had all hoped Smith Pritchett would be the one crowing on the courthouse steps.

Sergeant Hooker's voice crackled over the portable radio. "Savoy, Mullen, Prejean, Broussard, move in front of those goddamn reporters. Establish some distance between the crowd and Kudrow and Renard before this turns into a goddamn cluster fuck."

Annie edged her way between bodies, her hand resting on the butt of her baton, her eyes on Renard as Kudrow began to speak. He stood beside his attorney looking uncomfortable with the attention being focused on him. He wasn't a man to draw notice. Quiet, unassuming, an architect in the firm of Bowen & Briggs. Not ugly, not handsome. Thinning brown hair neatly combed and hazel eyes that seemed a little too big for their sockets. He stood with his shoulders stooped and his chest sunken, a younger shadow of his attorney. His mother stood on the step above him, a thin woman with a startled expression and a mouth as tight and straight as a hyphen.

"Some people will call this ruling a travesty of justice," Kudrow said loudly. "The only travesty of justice here has been perpetrated by the Partout Parish sheriff's department. Their *investigation* of my client has been nothing short of harassment. Two proir searches of Mr. Renard's home produced nothing that might tie him to the murder of Pamela Bichon."

"Are you suggesting the sheriff's department manipuilated evidence?" a reporter called out.

"Mr. Renard has been the victim of a narrow and fanatical investigation led by Detective Nick Fourcade. Y'all are aware of Fourcade's record with the New Orleans police department, of the reputation he brought with him to this parish. Detective Fourcade *allegedly* found that ring in my client's home. Draw you own conclusions."

As she elbowed past a television cameraman, Annie could see Fourcade turning around, half a dozen steps down from Kudrow. The cameras focused on him hastily. His expression was a stone mask, his eyes hidden by a pair of mirrored sunglasses. A cigarette smoldered between his lips. His temper was a thing of legend. Rumors abounded through the department that he was not quite sane.

He said nothing in answer to Kudrow's insinuation, and yet the air between them seemed to thicken. Anticipation held the crowd's breath. Fourcade pulled the cigarette from his mouth and flung it down, exhaling smoke through his nostrils. Annie took a half step toward Kudrow, her fingers curling around the grip of her baton. In the next heartbeat Fourcade was bounding up the steps—straight at Marcus Renard, shouting, "NO!"

"He'll kill him!" someone shrieked.

"Fourcade!" Hooker's voice boomed as the fat sergeant lunged after him, grabbing at and missing the back of his shirt.

"You killed her! You killed my baby girl!"

The anguished shouts tore from the throat of Hunter Davidson, Pamela Bichon's father, as he hurled himself down the steps at Renard, his eyes rolling, one arm swinging wildly, the other hand clutching a .45.

Fourcade knocked Renard aside with a beefy shoulder, grabbed Davidson's wrist and shoved it skyward as the .45 barked out a shot and screams went up all around. Annie hit Davidson from the right side, her much smaller body colliding with his just as Fourcade threw his weight against the man from the left. Davidson's knees buckled and they all went down in a tangle of arms and legs, grunting and shouting, bouncing hard down the steps, Annie at the bottom of the heap. Her breath was pounded out of her as she hit the concrete steps with four-hundred pounds of men on top of her.

"He killed her!" Hunter Davidson sobbed, his big body going limp. "He butchered my girl!"

Annie wriggled out from under him and sat up, grimacing. All she could think was that no physical pain could compare with what this man must have been enduring.

Swiping back the strands of dark hair that had pulled loose from her ponytail, she gingerly brushed over the throbbing knot on the back of her head. Her fingertips came away sticky with blood.

"Take this," Fourcade ordered in a low voice, thrusting Davidson's gun at Annie butt-first. Frowning, he leaned down over Davidson and put a hand on the man's shoulder even as Prejean snapped the cuffs on him. "I'm sorry," he murmured. "I wish I could'a let you kill him."

The author of the national bestseller *Dangerous to Hold* once again combines intoxicating passion with spellbinding suspense . . .

He'd sworn to protect her with his life.

THE BRIDE'S BODYGUARD
BY ELIZABETH THORTON

"A major, major talent . . . [a] superstar."—*Rave Reviews*

With his striking good looks, Ross Trevenan was one of the most attractive men Tessa Lorimer had ever seen. But five minutes in his company convinced her he was the most arrogant, infuriating man alive. That's why it was such a shock to discover Trevenan's true purpose: hired to escort her out of Paris and back to England, he had sworn that he'd do anything to keep her safe—even if he had to marry her to do it. Now, finding herself a bride to a devastatingly attractive bodyguard seems more hazardous than any other situation she could possibly encounter. Yet Tessa doesn't know that she holds the key to a mystery that Trevenan would sell his soul to solve . . . and a vicious murderer would kill to keep.

A movement on the terrace alerted Ross to the presence of someone else.

"Paul?"

Tessa's voice. Ross threw his cheroot on the ground and crushed it under his heel.

"Paul?" Her voice was breathless, uncertain. "I saw you from my window. I wasn't sure it was you until I saw our signal."

Ross said nothing, but he'd already calculated that he'd stumbled upon the trysting place of Tessa and her French lover and had inadvertently given their signal merely by smoking a cheroot.

Tessa entered the gazebo and halted, waiting for her eyes to become accustomed to the gloom. "Paul, stop playing games with me. You know you want to kiss me."

It never crossed Ross's mind to enlighten her about his identity. He was too curious to see how far the brazen hussy would go.

Her hands found his shoulders. "Paul," she whispered, and she lifted her head for his kiss.

It was exactly as she had anticipated. His mouth was firm and hot, and those pleasant sensations began to warm her blood. When he wrapped his arms around her and jerked her hard against his full length, she gave a little start of surprise, but that warm, mobile mouth on hers insisted she yield to him. She laughed softly when he kissed her throat, then she stopped breathing altogether when he bent her back and kissed her breasts, just above the lace on her bodice. He'd never gone that far before.

She should stop him, she knew she should stop him, but she felt as weak as a kitten. She said something—a protest? a plea?—and his mouth was on hers again, and everything Tessa knew about men and their passions was reduced to ashes in the scorching heat of that embrace. Her limbs were shaking, wild tremors shook her body, her blood seemed to ignite. She was clinging to him for support, kissing him back, allowing those bold hands of his to wander at will from her breast to her thigh, taking liberties she knew no decent girl should permit, not even a French girl.

When he left her mouth to kiss her ears, her eyebrows, her cheeks, she got out on a shaken whisper, "I never knew it could be like this. You make me feel things I never knew existed. You seem so different tonight."

And he did. His body was harder, his shoulders seemed broader, and she hadn't known he was so tall. As for his fragrance—

Then she knew, she *knew*, and she opened her eyes wide, trying to see his face. It was too dark, but she didn't need a light to know whose arms she was in. He didn't wear cologne as Paul did. He smelled of fresh air and soap and freshly starched linen.

"Trevenan!" she gasped, and fairly leapt out of his arms.

He made no move to stop her, but said in a laconic tone, "What a pity. And just when things were beginning to turn interesting."

She was so overcome with rage, she could hardly find her voice. "*Interesting?* What you did to me was not interesting. It was *depraved.*"

The lights on the terrace had yet to be extinguished, and she had a clear view of his expression. He could hardly keep a straight face.

"That's not the impression you gave me," he said. "I could have sworn you were enjoying yourself."

"I thought you were Paul," she shouted. "How dare you impose yourself on me in that hateful way."

He arched one brow. "My dear Miss Lorimer, as I recall, you were the one who imposed yourself on me. I was merely enjoying a quiet smoke when you barged into the gazebo and cornered me." His white teeth gleamed. "Might I give you a word of advice? You're too bold by half. A man likes to be the hunter. Try, if you can, to give the impression that *he* has cornered *you*."

She had to unclench her teeth to get the words out. "There is no excuse for your conduct. You knew I thought you were Paul."

"Come now. That trick is as old as Eve."

Anger made her forget her fear, and she took a quick step toward him. "Do you think I'd want your kisses? You're nothing but my grandfather's lackey. You're a secretary, an employee. If I were to tell him what happened here tonight," she pointed to the gazebo, "he would dismiss you."

"Tell him, by all means. He won't think less of me for acting like any red-blooded male. It's your conduct that will be a disappointment to him." His voice took on a hard edge. "By God, if I had the schooling of you, you'd learn to obey me."

"Thank God," she cried out, "that will never come to pass."

He laughed. "Stranger things have happened."

She breathed deeply, trying to find her calm. "If I'd known you were in the gazebo, I would never have entered it." His skeptical look revived her anger, and said, "I tell you, I thought you were Paul Marmont."

He shrugged. "In that case, all I can say is that little girls who play with fire deserve to get burned."

She raged, "You were teaching me a lesson?"

"In a word, yes."

Her head was flung back and she regarded him with smoldering dislike. "And just how far were you prepared to go in this lesson of yours, Mr. Trevenan? Mmm?"

He extended a hand to her, and without a trace of mockery or levity answered, "Come back to the gazebo with me and I'll show you."

In the bestselling tradition of Barbara Delinsky, an enthralling, emotionally charged novel of friendship, betrayal, forgiveness and love.

Jean Stone
PLACES BY THE SEA

Glamorous newswoman Jill McPhearson's past is calling her back . . . to an island, a house, a life she wants only to forget. Putting her childhood home on Martha's Vineyard in order takes all Jill's strength, but it will also give this savvy reporter her biggest break: the chance to go after the story of a lifetime . . . her own.

By the time she reached the end of Water Street, Jill realized where she had come. The lighthouse stood before her. The lighthouse where she'd spent so many hours, months, years, with Rita, thinking, dreaming, hoping.

She climbed down the dunes and found the path that led to their special place. Perhaps she'd find an answer here, perhaps she'd find some understanding as to what she had just read.

On the rocks, under the pier, what she found, instead, was Rita.

Jill stared at the back of the curly red hair. On the ground beside Rita stood a half-empty bottle of scotch. The ache in Jill's heart began to quiet, soothed by the comforting presence of her best friend—her once, a long time ago, best friend. She brushed her tears away and took another step.

"Care to share that bottle with an old friend?" she asked. "May I join you?"

Rita shrugged. "Last time I checked, it was still a free country."

Jill hesitated a moment. She didn't need Rita's caustic coldness right now. What she needed was a friend.

She hesitated a moment, then stooped beside her friend. "I thought maybe you'd be glad to see me."

Rita laughed. "Sorry. I was just too darned busy to roll out the red carpet."

Jill settled against a rock and faced Rita.

"Are you still angry at me for leaving the island?"

Rita stared off toward Chappy. "If I remember correctly, I left before you did."

"Where did you go, Rita? Why did you leave?"

Picking up the bottle of scotch, Rita took a swig. She held it a moment, then passed it to Jill without making eye contact. "Why did it surprise you that I left? You were the one who always said what a shithole this place was. You were the one who couldn't wait to get out of here."

Jill looked down the long neck of the bottle, then raised it to her lips. "But you were the one who wanted to stay."

Rita shrugged again. "Shit happens."

She handed the bottle back. "I've missed you."

A look of doubt bounced from Rita to Jill. "How long has it been? Twenty-five years? Well you missed me so much I never even got a Christmas card."

"My mother never told me you'd come back."

"That's no surprise. You should have guessed, though. You always thought I was destined to rot in this place."

Reaching out, Jill touched Rita's arm. Rita pulled away.

Jill took back her hand and rested it in her lap. "I was trying to make a new life for myself."

"And a fine job you did. So what is it now, Jill? Going to be another of the island's celebrities who graces us with your presence once a year?"

"No I'm selling the house."

Rita laughed. "See what I mean? You don't care about it here. You don't care about any of us. You never did."

A small wave lapped the shore. "Is that what you think?"

"You always thought I'd wind up like my mother. Well, in a lot of ways I guess I did. That should make you happy."

"Rita . . . I never meant . . . "

Rita's voice was slow, deliberate. "Yes you did. You were smarter than me, Jill. Prettier. More ambitious. I guess that's not a crime."

"It is if I hurt you that badly."

"You didn't hurt me, Jill. Pissed me off, maybe. But, no, you didn't hurt me."

Jill remembered Rita's laughter, Rita's toughness, and that Rita had always used these defenses to hide her insecurities, to hide her feelings that she wasn't as good as the kids who lived in the houses with mothers and fathers, the kids with dinner waiting on the table and clean, pressed clothes in their closets.

The heat of the sun warmed her face. "Life doesn't always go the way we want," she said. "No matter how hard we try."

Rita pulled her knees to her chest. "No shit."

The sound of a motor boat approached. They

both turned to watch as it shot through the water, white foam splashing, leaving a deep "V" of a wake.

"I can't believe you still come here," Jill said.

"Not many other places to think around here," Rita answered. "Especially in August." She hugged her knees, and looked at Jill. "I was real sorry about your parents. Your dad. Your mother."

"Thanks."

"I went to the service. For your mother."

Jill flicked her gaze back to the lighthouse, to the tourists. "I was in Russia," she said, aware that her words sounded weak, because Rita would know the real reason Jill hadn't returned had nothing to do with Russia. "Is your mother still . . ."

"Hazel?" Rita laughed. "Nothing's going to kill her. Found herself a man a few years ago. They live in Sarasota now."

Jill nodded. "That's nice. She's such a great person."

Rita plucked the bottle again and took another drink. "Yeah, well, she's different."

Closing her eyes, Jill let the sun soothe her skin, let herself find comfort in the sound of Rita's voice, in the way her words danced with a spirit all their own—a familiar, safe dance that Jill had missed for so long. "I've never had another best friend, Rita," she said, her eyes still closed to the sun, her heart opening to her friend.

Rita didn't reply.

Jill sat up and checked her watch. "I'd love to have you meet my kids," she said. "In fact, I have to pick up my daughter now." She hesitated a moment, then heard herself add, "Would you like to come?"

Rita paused for a heartbeat, or maybe it was two. "What time is it?"

"Five-thirty."

"I've got to start work at six. I tried to quit, but Charlie wouldn't let me. I'm a waitress there. At the tavern. Like my mother was."

"Tell Charlie he can live without you for one night," Jill said. "Come with me, Rita. Please."

Rita seemed to think about it. "What the hell," she finally said. "Why not."

The sun seemed to smile; the world seemed to come back into focus. "Great," Jill said, as she rose to her feet. "We've got so much to catch up on. First, though, we have to go back to my house and get the car. Amy's out at Gay Head."

"The car?" Rita asked.

Jill brushed off her shorts. "Hopefully, the workmen or any of their friends haven't boxed me in. I'm having some work done on the house and it's a power-saw nightmare."

"I'll tell you what," Rita said as she screwed the cap on the bottle. "You get the car. I'll wait here."

Jill didn't understand why Rita didn't want to come to the house, but, then Rita was Rita, and she always was independent. "Don't go away," she said as she waved good-bye and headed toward the road, realizing then that she hadn't asked Rita if she had ever married, or if she had any kids.

She was in the clear. At least about Kyle, Rita was in the clear.

She stared across the water and hugged her arms around herself. Jill had never known why Rita had left the Vineyard; she'd never known that Rita had been pregnant. Her secret was safe for now, safe forever.

And Jesus, it felt good to have a friend again.

On sale in April:

MISCHIEF

by Amanda Quick

ONCE A WARRIOR

by Karyn Monk